THE LAST RITE : SHORT BITES

Vol. 1
Bloodlines

by

Chad Robert Morgan

Copyright © 2023 Spectral Ink Productions

All rights reserved.

For Alex

CONTENTS

1 Race the Night 1

2 Almost Home 59

3 Family 117

4 Epilogue 167

RACE THE NIGHT

Angelo waited outside in the warm afternoon air, sitting on an old log and drawing in the dirt with a stick. He tried to draw maps of the world on the ground from memory, but the land masses didn't look right to him. He wished he had a globe like at school. He asked his mother for one, but she didn't know where to buy one. His mother was entertaining one of the foreigners again. She did that often. His mother – his *nanay* - said they were from far away, alone, and needed a friend for the night. That was her job to be a friend. Angelo wished he could help. He could be a friend too, but his mother said adults wanted adult friends. She said if there was ever a little boy needing a friend, Angelo would be the man for the job. In the meantime, though, he stayed outside and let his mother do her work.

Angelo asked his mother why the foreigners came to Angeles City in the Philippines. They were almost always men from places like Australia and America. He looked at them on a globe. They were very far away. His mother said people liked to travel, to meet new people. He wished he could travel. He would love to meet new people. He wanted to visit every country in the world when he grew up.

Their house was at the city's edge, in the weird in-between area where it faded into the jungle. The jungle used to scare him when he was little, but he was a big boy of five now. The jungle wasn't scary at all. Well, maybe a little at night, but during the day, it was nothing. Just a lot of trees and . . .

Someone was standing in the jungle looking at him. At first, he seemed blurry, and Angelo squinted to make him out. It must have been the sunlight coming through the humid air because the man came into focus. "*Tito* Marcus?"

His uncle strolled out of the trees like he was stepping out of his bedroom. He was dressed all in white, which wasn't too strange for the Philippines. It was always warm, and the light color reflected heat, or so his mom told him. "Hello, Angelo. How are you?"

Angelo got to his feet. "What are you doing here?"

"I came to see you," his *tito* said. "Your *nanay* busy again?"

Angelo nodded knowingly. "She's working."

"I figured," his *tito* said. "Why don't you come home with me? I'll make you some *turon*."

Angelo smacked his lips. He did love *turon*, the thin slices of banana and brown sugar wrapped in *lumpia* and fried until it was crispy. His *tito* made *turon* like no one else. He could sell it to the western tourists, but he didn't like tourists. He said they were rude and pushy, though they were always nice to his mother. He looked over his shoulder at the house where his mother entertained a traveler. She always told him not to interrupt her while she was with a client.

"It's okay," his *tito* said as if reading his mind. "Your mother won't mind. I told her I was coming for you."

He looked from his uncle to the house his mother was in. It felt wrong to leave without telling his mother where he was going, but if his uncle said it was okay, it should be fine. His uncle outstretched his hand, and after a moment of hesitation, Angelo took it.

But *Tito* Marcus didn't lead him down the streets toward the city center where his apartment was. He led Angelo into the jungle.

"Where are we going?" Angelo asked.

"It's a surprise." His uncle smiled down at him. "You trust me?"

Angelo nodded and let his *tito* guide him deep into the jungle. He didn't see the wide, toothy grin on his *tito's* face.

"Eat up, May," her *tita* Hiraya said.

It took May a moment to realize her *tita* was talking to her, that she was May. She wasn't always May. For that matter, her *tita* wasn't always Hiraya. She was still getting used to calling her *tita* – her aunt - by her new identity. She still thought of her *tita* by her old name and had to translate, not unlike when converting what was said by the

English-speaking foreigners to her native Tagalog in her head. When they left the village she had lived in all her life, her *tita* said they needed to be new people. It was easy to reinvent themselves in Angeles City. It was much larger than her old village, with people constantly coming and going. People often didn't stay for long, either foreigners visiting the city's famous nightlife or young girls trying to earn as much money from them as possible while they were still young and beautiful. Two more people entering the city went unnoticed. It didn't matter that their names were fictitious. No one cared.

Did she like being May? It was hard to say. May had grown much more popular than she had been in her old life, but those people didn't really know her. It just meant she and her *tita* were accomplished in hiding the monster she really was, the monster deep inside her. How long had she been May? She was already losing count. The days melded together when you had an infinite number of them to look forward to.

May stared at her plate. Once upon a time, she loved *sinangag*, especially how her *tita* made it mixed with bits of fried sausage that paired well with the garlic. Once, the smell of it made her mouth water. That was before the black thing infested her. Now it nauseated her. Everything smelled like bile and rot to her because of the black thing. She forced herself to take a bite, and her stomach churned. Her *tita* looked on in disapproval.

"You need to keep your body alive if we ever hope to get the black chick out of you and make you human again," her *tita* snarled. May didn't take it personally. She couldn't remember her *tita* smiling a day in her natural life. Or her unnatural one, for that matter.

May let out an exasperated sigh. She didn't know if she would ever get the black thing out of her, the thing her mother passed on to her, the thing that made her no longer human. Her *tita* was right. If she didn't eat, her human body would die. Then she would be completely reliant on the black thing to survive, which is what it wanted. That was why the sinister little thing made regular food so distasteful for her. She took a bite, ignoring the rancid taste, but no sooner did she swallow than her stomach tried to puke it back up. May clenched her mouth shut and forced it back down. Her stomach churned in protest, but she kept it down.

"Come on," her *tita* said. "Your mother managed to stomach that for nine months."

May forced down another bite. She had no idea how her mother managed to do it for nine minutes, let alone nine months. When her mother was pregnant with May, the fetus needed real food to grow. She felt sick the entire time, according to her mother. For nine months.

"How long will I have to keep from vomiting every meal?" May wondered out loud. "Nine months? Nine years? Nine decades?"

Her *tita* sat down at the table with her own plate, her wrinkled face staring at May as she started eating. She said nothing to May as she chewed. She didn't need to. Her glare said it all. May slammed her hands onto the table and stood up.

"You aren't done eating," her *tita* said.

"Yes, I am," May said.

"You saw what happened to your mother when the black thing

was removed," her *tita* said. "If you want to survive when we remove the black thing-"

"We're never removing the black thing!" May snapped. "I'm damned! Cursed! No one has ever removed the black thing and lived!"

"No one we know of," her *tita* Hiraya said.

"No one *it* knows of!" May shouted. "I know everything the black thing knows, and it has never seen anyone survive once it was removed!"

"We can't give up hope," her *tita* said. "I've lived long enough to know things change. We used to try to cure appendicitis with chicken gizzards. Now we have surgeons and antibiotics. We learn, and we improve over time, and that is something we both have. You just need to be patient."

"Easy for you to say," May said. "How would you feel if you had to eat spoiled meat for the rest of your life? Because that's what it tastes like to me now, like it's all rotten and disgusting." She pounded her chest. "This is my life now! A never-ending cycle of being violently ill, either from the food I can no longer stomach or by the acts I have to commit to feed the black thing!"

"We will find a way to make you human again." Her *tita* spoke in an uncharacteristically calm voice, making May think of a tiger readying to pounce. Not long ago, before she became May, that tone of voice would have terrified her, but May wasn't that young girl anymore.

"I'll never be human again!" she shouted. "I'm a monster!"

"You are not defined by that dark thing inside you," her aunt said in a forced calm. "You are only a monster if you surrender to it."

"And how long am I supposed to resist?" May asked.

"For as long as it takes," her *tita* said.

She knew her *tita* was right, but she felt the weight of immortality on her shoulders. Her *tita* lived a supernaturally long life herself, but unlike her *tita*, May would never age. The person she was today would be the same person she would be tomorrow, and the next day, and the next day, never changing like a marble statue. The concept of living for centuries was new for May. They were at opposite ends of the same road, and seeing the endless journey before her was exhausting and disheartening. Frustrated, she turned and left the house, slamming the door behind her.

The modest house they shared was on the edge of the city. When she and her *tita* first came to the city, they set up in a small apartment near the bars and hotels. The services they provided for the women of Angeles City, however beneficial they may be, were illegal. Keeping their operations from being discovered so near the heart of the city was challenging. Too many passers-by, too many lights. Moving to the city's edge meant fewer people, fewer police, and fewer witnesses.

She walked the streets a lot. Not that the city was so scenic – some of it was downright disgusting – but she had a lot of time. She was immortal and had no need to sleep. She wondered how many centuries would go by before the boredom of the never-ending days made her go insane. Besides, she sometimes found positive uses for her dark gifts, patrolling the city like some sort of vigilante and rescuing people in need. Every person she helped eased her conscience just a little bit more.

The village she grew up in was lined with pineapple groves on one end and jungle on the other. She would walk hours to the closest town to shop at the market, but even that town was nothing compared to the massive urban sprawl of Angeles City. When she first arrived, May was amazed at the endless rows of homes, shops, and, above all, bars where the young girls hung out. The air was humid and thick, just like at home, but it trapped the exhaust from the legions of vehicles crisscrossing the city like ants crawling over a dead rat.

No, that wasn't a fair comparison. Ants would have been more organized.

The result was a sky tinged brown and thick with diesel fumes. May missed the clean air of her village and the sweet smell of the pineapples during harvest season. The city reeked of petroleum and discarded food rotting in the island heat, made worse by her heightened senses.

As May walked down the street, she was aware of the eyes on her. The women were either grateful to her or condemned her for her work, and the men all desired her. It was one of the gifts of the black thing, her physical attributes molded and accentuated to make her stunningly beautiful. It was a gift not worth the price.

Seeing the scorn on the faces of some of the women didn't bother her. In her old village, back when she was still human, she was a pariah. She was the niece of the *mangkukulam* – a witch – so everyone in the village looked down at her. Like now, they were too scared to cross them, afraid of what retribution would entail, so May didn't pay them any mind. What was odd, what she was uncomfortable with, were those that looked at her with admiration. Many were grateful for May's help, though she wondered if they would feel the same if they knew the form that help came in. May was disgusted with herself for what she had to do to feed the black thing inside her, but it was a small consolation knowing she put such horrible talents to good use.

Smells from the street vendors fought to overpower the stench of burnt diesel fuel. May missed being human, missed salivating over the *kamote q* or *tonkneneng* or especially fish balls. Oh, how she used to love the balls of fried dough, trying them with different dipping sauces. Now the smells of the human food made her stomach churn. The black thing gave her immortality, but what good was it if even the simpler pleasures of life were denied to her?

Many of the houses were made of bare cinderblocks, a durable material that could withstand some of the island storms. This was a more affluent area of the city, but even here, there were sheds made of scraps in the alleys. May would often see a dirty face poke out of a doorway with only a blanket for a door or a mother washing a child in a bucket of collected rainwater. Children would play in the streets, making a game of throwing their sandals into a tin can. This was the Philippines. There was no welfare. The public schools were so full they taught classes in shifts. If you had no family, your survival and that of your children were up to you.

Sitting on the ground at the entrance of an alley was a woman so starved that May could make out the outline of every bone in her body. She held a tiny infant to her chest. It was skin and bones with a belly like an inflated ball, with no sign of what gender it was. It didn't have the energy to suckle on its mother's breast but dangled from its mother's arm as if dead. The black thing inside her stirred, smelling the untarnished purity and life the infant still held. It whispered to May that letting the black thing have the baby would be a mercy, feeding May its desires and hunger.

Stop it, May thought to it. She didn't know if the black thing understood her thoughts as language. Still, it seemed to understand her intention easily enough. Even as it growled back, she mentally shouted, *I keep you well-fed. You don't need this child.*

It was easy to suppress the cravings of the dark thing when she kept it so well fed, much easier than when it was starving. May knelt and handed the mother a few pesos. The emaciated woman didn't have the strength to take it, so May put the money in her hand and closed her fingers around it. The mother blinked and looked up at her.

"Are you here to take my baby?" the mother asked, a tear running down her face.

May thought, *Does she know who I am? What I am?*

The black thing inside her hissed with gluttonous desire but May ignored it again. "Do you want me to?"

The mother held her child closer to her chest and shook her head. "No."

"Then I won't," May smiled. She caressed the baby's bald head. "I'll ask my *tita* to come and see you. She might be able to help and might have some medicine. In the meantime, take the money and get some food."

The mother cried more. "Thank you."

May smiled and left the mother with her child. She was a bit envious of her *tita*. Before the Spanish came and branded her a witch, she was a medicine woman using folk remedies to treat the people of her village. All May could do was take life. If that was all she was suitable for, she could at least try to use her skills in a way that would help instead of hurt.

May continued down the street, aiming toward the center of the city. Houses gave way to shops, cafes, and other places of business. She liked this area of the city, far away from the bars and nightclubs that were the city's main draw but busier and livelier than the rows of houses. It reminded her of the town she would walk to from the village to do her shopping. Back then, she dreamed of moving to the town, escaping her village and all those who looked down upon her, and becoming invisible. That town was barely larger than the village she wanted to run from when compared to Angeles City. Still, even here, she found that becoming invisible was impossible. Wherever she went, she felt eyes on her.

Sitting at a table on the porch of a café was a western tourist and a *pinay* woman. The man had a youthful face, but his silver hair gave his age away. The woman with him could have been young enough to be his daughter, with long black hair and beautiful brown skin. That was typical for Angeles City, where Western men came to meet Filipina women. Sometimes they came looking for a wife. Most times, they came looking for a date for the weekend. Either way, such a couple was ordinary for Angeles City. However, these two made the hairs on the back of her neck stand on end for some reason. As she walked by, she turned her head to look at them. The couple shifted their attention to their meal, only to glance back at her a moment later.

May didn't have time to puzzle it out. One of her former patients came running toward her. Nenita had been pregnant with her third child, but the pregnancy had gone horribly wrong. To save Nenita's life, May had to take the life of her unborn child, something the black thing inside her did with relish. Not that Nenita ever saw that. Before May morphed into the monster she was and sucked the damaged fetus from the womb, her *tita* put Nenita into a deep sleep. All Nenita knew was when she woke up, her life was no longer in jeopardy. Since that day, Nenita usually greeted May with gratitude and joy whenever they met, but today her eyes were wide in panic. She called out to May and took her hand, too breathless to say anything.

"What's wrong?" May asked.

Nenita gasped for air as she tried to speak while she dragged May behind her. "Tala! Her son! Hurry, please!"

May ran with Nenita without effort. She could have run laps around Nenita and not break a sweat, but she had no idea where she was going. She also didn't want to expose her supernatural talents. Best to let everyone believe she was still human.

Nenita led May to where a small crowd was gathering. In the center of the cluster of people was Tala, tears running down her face. Her makeup, something Tala undoubtedly spent considerable time to make perfect, was ruined. As it ran down her face, it made her look like she was melting. She was on the verge of hysterics, straining to maintain an ounce of sanity. Everyone was shouting over each other to be heard.

"Calm, please," May said, using *the voice*, another of the black thing's gifts. Hearing her, the crowd fell silent. Even Tala stopped her frantic screaming, though the tears still flowed. The crowd parted for her as May walked to Tala and took her hands. "What's wrong?"

"Angelo is missing," Tala said. "I can't find him anywhere."

"It's okay," May said, using her hypnotic voice the black thing granted her to keep Tala calm. "We will find him. Tell me, where was the last place you saw him."

Tala gulped down a tear. "Outside our house. I was with a client."

May nodded. Everyone knew what she meant. It was a career many young women in Angeles City held, entertaining the western men - primarily Australian but many Americans and some Europeans - who came to Angeles City for that purpose. Many left children behind as they went home, never to be seen again. It also wasn't uncommon for the children of such hostesses to wander the city unsupervised. Angelo was one of the more fortunate ones, having a mother that cared for him, and a home not fashioned out of scrap.

"Take me to where you last saw him," May said.

Tala led the way. May followed Tala, and the crowd followed May. Tala took them to her house, sitting in that in-between state of city and jungle. May could see Angelo's footprints in the dirt with her heightened senses. From the jungle came a second set that looked odd, though May couldn't say why. Something smelled wrong too, but picking out the scent with the all the car exhaust was hard. She couldn't investigate closer with all the people around. She turned to the crowd.

"Let's spread out and start searching," she said, using *the voice* to encourage their obedience.

The crowd broke into smaller groups, obeying May's command and spreading out in all directions calling out Angelo's name. That left May alone with Tala. May followed the tracking a few feet into the jungle and knelt. She could see Angelo's small footprints walking off, but the other set shifted. Walking away with Angelo, they looked human. In fact, they looked too human, too perfectly formed. Before that, though, the prints were malformed. The further back they went, the less human they looked. Far enough back, and they no longer looked like feet. More like . . . hooves.

"I don't know what I'll do if anything happens to my Angelo," Tala said, more to herself than to May. "I didn't think I'd even want kids, but then . . ."

Tala trailed off, lost in thought and regret. May finished her sentence for her. "Then you got pregnant with Angelo."

"No," Tala said. "I was first pregnant at fourteen. I was so scared. I couldn't work while pregnant. No one would hire me. I had no family. I could barely feed myself. How could I feed a baby? It was scary, but it was also a bit exciting. Someone was growing inside me, someone I could care for and love. I can still remember the names I picked out. If it was a girl, Bituin. For a boy, Maliksi."

May could hear the bittersweet emotions swirling in her voice.

She'd seen it time and time again as patients agonized over a decision that, once made, could never be unmade, even in those cases when there was no choice to be had. Tala was staring off at an alternate life where her first child lived, seeing an older sibling care for Angelo as she watched them both with love. Tears rolled down Tala's cheek, the life that never could be evaporating as reality reasserted itself. May had a feeling she knew where Tala's story was going. "What happened?"

Tala wiped snot from her nose with the back of her hand. "The pregnancy made me sick. I could barely get out of bed. My stomach felt like I was stabbed with knives. Maybe I wasn't eating enough. Like I said, I could barely feed myself back then. I was almost a kid myself. There was a woman who gave me medicine. This was before you came. The woman said the medicine would make it go away. It made me bleed for days. I almost died. Can you imagine? Either dying because you are pregnant or dying trying to save yourself? Afterward, I felt so bad for what I had done."

It was an all-too-familiar story. May had heard it a hundred times. She used her dark talents to try to stop it from happening again. Most people had no appreciation of how dangerous pregnancy could be. Occasionally, something went so wrong with the fetus that it could kill the mother if the pregnancy didn't end. In the Philippines, such procedures were illegal no matter the reasons, so women were left with a difficult choice. For many, the cure was worse than the disease. If they survived, they risked jail time if they were ever discovered.

"Maybe I shouldn't have done it," Tala whimpered, almost to herself instead of to May. "Maybe I don't deserve to be a mother."

"You didn't have a choice," May said. "If you died, the baby would have died with you anyway. It happens. More often than you might think. Almost three thousand times a year, in fact."

"Maybe. All I know was, once the baby was gone, I missed it." Tala cocked her head. "Is that weird? Missing a baby that was never born?"

"No," May said. "No, it isn't."

"I didn't know if I would have another chance after that," Tala said. "I didn't know if I wanted to have kids, but the idea that I couldn't . . . I felt like I was damaged. I was worried. What if all that bleeding broke me?"

May knew it didn't work like that. Tala was lucky to be alive. The bleeding she experienced could have killed her or led to an infection that would have been slower but no less lethal. However, the bleeding Tala experienced, as scary as it was, wasn't likely to have damaged her ability to have babies in the future.

Despite the tears, Tala began to smile. "I hadn't meant to get pregnant with Angelo, but I was happy when I was. I thought of it as my second chance, to make up for the one I couldn't keep. I thought, maybe God forgave me. And now I've lost him too . . ."

Tala broke down into tears, collapsing to her knees as she sobbed. May walked out of the forest and knelt in front of her. Lifting Tala's head to face her own, May said, "We will find him."

"Maybe God is punishing me for my sins," Tala wept.

"Bad things happen to good and bad people alike," May said. "I don't think God had anything to do with this. And even if he did, if he wanted to punish you for doing what you needed to do to survive in his world, he shouldn't have made it so damn hard."

She resisted using *the voice* on Tala. She wanted Tala to be calm and reassured, but not because May hypnotized her. May wanted Tala to believe Angelo would come home safe because it was the truth. Tala nodded and forced a smile.

May got back to her feet and twisted to face the jungle. May didn't recognize the scent, but the black thing did. She knew what took Angelo.

"Tikbalang?" May's *tita* asked. "Haven't seen one of those in ages. Thought they had gone extinct."

"So did the black thing," May nodded, not looking at her *tita* but out the west-facing window, watching the sun get low in the sky. She couldn't chase after the *tikbalang* until nightfall. If it wasn't for the memories of the black thing inside her, she would have thought the *tikbalang* was nothing but a myth. Then again, she was a monster of myth herself. "Here's what confuses me. What would bring a t*ikbalang* so close to the city to take a small boy? They prefer the mountains and jungles away from humans."

"They have been known to lure humans into the jungle and attack them," her *tita* said.

"That's usually around their territory to scare off humans from wandering into their lairs," May said, reading the memories of the black thing as if they were her own. "They have a reputation for being mischievous but not outright malignant. This kind of abduction isn't their style. Why here? Why now? What does it want?"

"I can only think of one reason for taking a young boy," her *tita* said. "To feed."

The last rays of sunlight vanished behind the mountains. May readied herself. "It's time."

May left their house and headed away from the city lights, her *tita* in tow. She needed to be deep in the jungle, away from prying eyes, and where what she left behind would be safe. The black thing inside her wiggled in her gut, not hiding its agitation. May felt waves of fear and anger wash over her, begging her to stay home and ordering her not to pursue the *tikbalang*.

I wish you'd shut up, May thought to the black thing.

"You don't need to do this," her *tita* said. "This isn't your problem."

"I'm the only one who can help," May said. "The humans won't be fast enough. They'll never catch it."

"And if it catches you?" her *tita* asked. "You know what will happen if you don't return before sunrise."

"I have to try," May said.

"No, you don't," her *tita* growled. "That's my point. You're not listening, child. None of this concerns you."

May spun at her. "If I do nothing, then I truly am a monster. Is that what you want?"

"I want you to be safe," her *tita* said.

May began to undress. She learned the hard way how hard her transformation was on clothing. She hung her clothes on a nearby tree branch. "I'll be fine."

"You've never faced a *tikbalang*," her *tita* growled. "The black thing may have, in one of its previous hosts, but that's not the same as you facing one. They're fast, possibly even faster than you. This is dangerous." Her *tita* grabbed May by the arm. "Don't go."

May pealed her *tita's* fingers off her arm, stepped back, and began her transformation. First came the shifting of the black thing, the hard stone-like creature crawling up into her chest. It crawled under her still-beating heart. It hurt like hell, another of the black thing's passive effects to encourage her to let her human body die – no beating heart, no pain. The thumping of her heart against the rock-hard skin of the black thing was made worse as her body shifted fat, organs, and fluids down to her lower half. She was *aswang*, and her body was like clay, but even the *aswang* had to obey the laws of physics. She could reshape her body, but mass had to be maintained. Her body grew emaciated as matter was shifted to her back. Long, thin limbs grew from her shoulder blades, stretching out a thin membrane to form wings. Her fingernails thickened into long, sharp claws that glinted in the moonlight. At the same time, her teeth thinned and lengthened until she had a mouthful of fangs. Her legs melted together and hardened, roots growing out of what used to be her feet, and plunged deep into the ground, gripping the earth and anchoring herself. This was critical for the next part, which she hated the most. She began to flap her large batlike wings. As large as they were and as supernaturally strong as she was, the human body was too massive to take to the air. But if half of her mass was left behind . . .

Where the flesh of her stomach met the bark-like skin of her lower half, it began to rip. Blood trickled down the tree stump that was once her lower half, but she molded her body to seal the ripped blood vessels. May flapped harder, pulling herself up, snapping her intestines like rubber bands. The vertebrae in her back separated with a cacophony of popping tendons and nerves.

The black thing didn't speak in any language but conveyed thoughts, feelings, and sensations to May. Still, it made itself clear enough. *It hurts. The pain will end once you let your human body die.*

Go to hell, May thought to the black thing as she screamed in pain. Her body was ripped in half, and with her wings beating a steady rhythm, she took to the sky.

Angelo's *tito* took him nowhere near his home. He didn't think to question it for the first hour or so. His *tito* asked Angelo if he trusted him, and Angelo said he did. As his legs started to ache, he began to second-guess his *tito*. Stumbling through the jungle – Angelo stumbled, his *tito* walked as sure-footed as if he was in his own home – Angelo looked around for any landmarks he might recognize but found none. Just trees and more trees. Still, he said nothing. He was confused and wanted to ask when they would get to his *tito's* home, but they walked in silence. He trusted his *tito*.

When the sun set, however, panic displaced trust. The jungle had no limit to how dark it grew. It got dark around his mother's house, but even there, the glow of the bars and hotels pushed back against the night. Now, there was nothing but the moon.

Worse, his eyes played tricks on him in the dim light.

In the darkness, his *tito's* hair seemed to grow long like a girl's. His face looked stretched out, but that couldn't be right, could it? His *tito* held his hand, but as the sun sank behind the horizon, it began to feel different. His hand gripped Angelo's tighter, and he felt rough hair brushing against his wrist. Angelo caught the whiff of something like cigarettes, like what some of his mother's clients smoked but much stronger. Then they walked under a small hole in the tree canopy, and he saw his *tito* in silhouette against the full moon. His legs were shaped weirdly. They had an extra bend to them. Angelo screamed and yanked his arm, but he couldn't break his *tito's* grip – or whatever this thing was that pretended to be his *tito*.

The thing turned its long neck to Angelo, and he saw its horse-shaped head for the first time, framed by the silver moon. It glared at him with black, glossy eyes the size of baseballs. "Quiet."

Angelo screamed even louder.

"I said, be quiet!" the horse-monster growled. "If you yell one more time-"

The horse monster, the *tikbalang*, never finished his thought. Something fast and big swooped by it and sliced its opposite arm like a knife. The *tikbalang* howled in pain as its blood sprinkled on the ground. For a second, the hand gripping Angelo relaxed as it was about to reach for its wound out of reflex. Before Angelo could take advantage of it, the furry hand of the *tikbalang* clamped down. It felt like all the bones in his hand were about to snap. Then the *tikbalang* took off, nearly ripping his arm out of the socket. The *tikbalang* swept

Angelo into his arms, and he smelled the warm blood from its cut. The thing raced through the jungle at blinding speed, darting between trees and stepping over rocks effortlessly. It ran hunched over with an awkward three-legged gate, Angelo taking up one arm.

As scared as Angelo was of the *tikbalang*, what scared him more was the thing in the air after him. Anything scary enough to terrify a *tikbalang* was beyond Angelo's comprehension. He looked over the *tikbalang's* shoulder and up to the sky. As the gaps in the trees whipped by, he could catch glimpses of large bat-like wings flapping high in the sky. Angelo didn't think it could be any scarier.

Then it was gone.

Somehow that was worse. At least before, he knew where it was. Now, it could be anywhere, and there was no chance it just left. Angelo could hear branches snapping and leaves being slashed, but he couldn't tell if it was from the *tikbalang* or something worse.

The *tikbalang* arced to the left, and that was its mistake. The thing in the air made a tighter arc and intercepted the *tikbalang*, slicing the leg. The *tikbalang* fell, tumbling head over hoof. Angelo was tossed in the air and crashed into the forest floor.

Angelo was scared, he was cold, and now he was in pain. He began to cry. The more he cried, the more frightened he got knowing he was telling the monsters where he was, but he couldn't help himself. All that fear and pain needed to come out of him, and the more scared he got, the harder he cried.

Then he saw it. The thing from the air, only it wasn't in the air anymore. It was on the ground with him. It crawled with its wings toward him, dragging its lower half along the dirt. Two glowing green eyes looked at him, peering from a face shriveled up like a plum that had died on the tree. It reached out to him with a boney hand, and the tips of her fingers were long, sharp claws coated in the blood of the *tikbalang*.

He knew what the monster was. Every kid in the Philippines knew what it was and had nightmares about them.

The *manananggal*. The baby-eater.

"Angelo?" the *manananggal* said. "It's okay. Don't be scared."

Angelo was very scared. He screamed and screamed as the *manananggal* reached out to him. Before she could touch him, the *tikbalang* rammed into her, and the two vanished in a blur into the night. Angelo could only see glimpses of the two monsters as they fought – a flash of a wing, a blur of mane whipping by, a spray of blood. Part of Angelo wanted to run, but the total darkness of the jungle was just as terrifying to the young boy as the creatures trying to kill each other.

Then he was whisked off the ground. The *tikbalang* had him again, rushing between the trees, but Angelo could feel the uneven stride. The wind didn't whip by him as before. The creature was injured and tired but determined.

"I will not be robbed of my vengeance," the *tikbalang* gasped, then turned its head to the sky. Angelo heard it, too, the flapping of those bat-like wings. The *manananggal* was after them. The *tikbalang* darted to the side and pinned itself behind a tree. For a split second, Angelo forgot he was in the arms of a *tikbalang* and felt an ounce of relief as the *manananggal* soared past overhead. Then the *tikbalang* dropped him to the ground. Before he had time to realize he should be very, very afraid, the *tikbalang* stuck its horse face in his and opened its mouth wide. Angelo thought it would bite his head off with those large, square teeth, each looking like a domino, but then the *tikbalang* inhaled. The air between them glowed blue. It was the last thing he saw.

May lost it, lost the boy. Damn it.

Where did it go? she thought to the black thing inside her. The black thing, however, chose to stay silent. *Help me! Where did it go?*

The black thing replied in a cluster of sensations and feelings that equated to, *Why should I?*

If you don't help me, May thought, *I will rip you out of me and have my* tita *throw you in the sea where you will sink to the bottom and never be seen again!*

Images of her body shriveling in pain before turning to dust flashed in her mind, the dark thing's way of arguing back. They were her own memories of what happened to her mother when the black thing was passed to May.

I don't care, May thought back, ignoring her *tita's* effort to prevent that from happening to her. *It will be worth it if I die to get rid of you forever! So help me or spend eternity at the bottom of the ocean!*

The whole conversation, along with the black thing's consideration, went at the speed of thought. It was over in the time it took May to take a breath. By her next, May could sense something deep in the jungle below. The black thing was vague as to what it was – May suspected it could not adequately describe it in a way a human could understand – but she got the sense of something like a life force or a soul.

Angelo's soul.

The *tikbalang* was in its true form now. It stood tall and thin, one giant claw wrapped around Angelo's chest and pinning him to a tree. It was so pale it almost glowed in the night like the moon, illuminated by the blue aura it was sucking out of Angelo. From its head and down its back was a flowing mane of black. Flowing, that was, except for three stiff, thick hairs along its spine, almost like quills.

She dropped from the sky, gravity pulling her down faster and faster, using her wings only to steer. Her body crashed into it, knocking it off Angelo. The boy fell unconscious to the ground, and the *tikbalang* went into the air. May hit the ground herself, her wings wrapping around her body as she rolled uncontrollably until careening into a tree.

The jungle was still. The *tikbalang* lay unmoving. So did Angelo. May hurt all over, tangled up in her own broken wings. Pain shot through them as she unraveled herself and forced her snapped limbs to start knitting back together. She crawled with her claws toward Angelo, the bones in her wings being pulled back into place. She was a *manananggal*, an *aswang*. Her body was like clay, for her to mold as she saw fit.

May reached the small boy lying motionless on the ground. She caressed Angelo's cheek and sensed the blood coursing through his veins. His heartbeat was weak, but he was alive. She pulled him into her arms and began to flap. Damn, the boy was heavy, and it was already hard to get airborne once on the ground. Her wings could only flap half as much before slapping the jungle floor, reducing her lift. She needed height.

Holding the boy to her chest with one arm, she used her wings and her other arm to climb up the thickest tree she could find. She held herself on the tree with her one free hand, gripped the tree's bark with the sharp ends of her wings, pushed herself up, then quickly let go and reached higher in the tree. She repeated this over and over, each time getting a little higher and each time her arm growing a little weaker.

Something yanked her down. She grappled with her limbs to keep from falling out of the tree. Looking down, she saw the *tikbalang* on the ground, standing up to its full length and gripping her dangling entrails in one outstretched hand. May strained against the *tikbalang's* grip, trying to pull herself up the tree. Her entrails were slick with blood and bile, and they slipped out of the *tikbalang's* claw.

The *tikbalang* roared in anger. May didn't know if *tikbalangs* could climb, but May didn't hesitate. She kept climbing. Then the whole tree shook as the *tikbalang* slammed into it. She looked down to see the lanky creature dart away, only to ram back into the tree at full speed a second later. May guessed that meant that *tikbalangs* couldn't climb, so instead, it would knock the tree down or at least try to shake her out of it. As she continued her climb, she heard wood cracking at the tree's base. It began to lean, and May could feel the tree straining to stay upright in a fight against gravity it was losing. Its acceleration to the ground was boosted by each slam of the *tikbalang*. Soon, the tree was in freefall. It was now or never. Using the velocity of the falling tree, May leaped into the air and spread her wings, holding Angelo with both arms. She fell with the tree, struggling to clear its branches, but as the tree hit the ground, she shot past it, skirting the jungle floor.

She was in the air . . . barely. She fought to get altitude and speed. Each flap of the wings got her another inch in the air and got her just a little bit faster. Usually, she soared through the air effortlessly. Still, she had never had to carry something as heavy as a five-year-old. Then she heard the sound of hooves clopping after her, not the twin sets of a horse but the uneven bipedal gate of the injured *tikbalang*. Even injured, the thing was fast. Its stride was almost as long as her wingspan, the horse-like legs springing it forward with each step. It was gaining on her.

May didn't know if she could fly faster than the *tikbalang*, not with the extra weight of Angelo, but she could fly higher than it could reach. She climbed as fast as she could as the snorting of the *tikbalang* grew ever closer. She wouldn't look back. She just flew harder. From under her, she could feel its sharp claws trying to grip her dangling entrails. She pushed her body even harder, straining every muscle to climb out of its reach. She could feel the tips of its claws slashing at the end of a piece of intestine. Then, she could feel nothing but the air wafting against her as the *tikbalang's* claw missed over and over.

As she continued to climb, she chanced a look behind herself. The *tikbalang* stood there, staring back at her. Safe in the night sky, she was finally able to turn her attention to Angelo. With her enhanced vision, she could see how pale he was, even in the black of night. He shivered in her arms, breathing shallowly.

May slapped the boy's face. "Angelo? Wake up, Angelo. Talk to me."

The boy stirred. Then, realizing what was holding him, he tried to get away, but without the energy to do so. He surrendered to the *manananggal's* embrace and began to cry.

"It's okay," May said. "Don't be scared. I won't hurt you."

Angelo could only whimper in reply.

May caressed his hair. "Talk to me. Tell me what you want to do when you grow up."

Angelo mumbled through his tears, "I want to see all the countries in the world."

May kissed the boy's forehead, careful not to cut him with her razor-sharp teeth. "You will, Angelo. I swear it. You will."

The old woman stood by what looked like a tree stump, one that wasn't there a few hours ago. May's *tita* — her aunt — had changed her name many times throughout the years. People got suspicious when one didn't die, so she would move to a different place and take on a new identity every few decades. Her niece was struggling with this, but she was used to it. The irony was that until May was cursed with the black thing, she was starting to think she wouldn't have to do it again. The village, after years of fearing her, calling her a *mangkukulam* or worse, was beginning to trust her. They were starting to accept her for who she was. She didn't need to hide anymore.

Then the black thing leaped down her niece's throat. There

would be no place for her in the village any longer. It was time to move on and reinvent herself once again. In this city, she was known as Hiraya. It seemed fitting, as it meant "fruits of hope." These days, she was the only hope for her niece, now called May. She had to keep May's hope alive if there was any chance to get the black thing out of her niece without it killing her. It was a daily struggle. When each day was another step in an endless path, it was easy to surrender to despair. It was Hiraya's job to keep that from happening.

She heard her niece before she saw her, the flapping of her giant wings. She could tell from the long swooping noise that May was tired and under a heavy load. She must be carrying the boy. She gritted her teeth. They hadn't been here that long. They were already too public as May used her unnatural talents to help the women in the city. Rescuing the boy risked exposing her monstrous identity. It would suck to need to invent yet another new name so soon. She was just getting used to being Hiraya.

When May came over the treetops and lowered down to the tree trunk, Hiraya could see the boy in her arms, but he was very still. She creased her brow in concern. As May rested on the thing that looked like a tree stump, which was May's lower half, Hiraya could see how pale the boy looked, even in the moonlight.

The boy looked like he was fed upon.

There was a fleeting moment when Hiraya wondered if May had feasted on the boy, a thought that was gone in an instant while her shame in suspecting her niece lingered. Even if she didn't have faith in her niece's character or her ability to fight against the cravings of the dark thing inside her, it wasn't possible. The black thing needed its victims to be young and pure. The boy was too old to be a desirable meal for the *manananggal*. To the black thing, his life force would taste . . . stale? Spoiled? Still, taking the unmoving boy from May into her own arms, Hiraya could see the boy was ill. He was drained. Something had fed on the child. If it wasn't May, then what?

"The *tikbalang*?" Hiraya asked.

May nodded. Hiraya noticed her niece wasn't reforming with her lower half. May sat there with her wings wrapped around herself like a cloak. "Can you help him?"

Hiraya looked at the boy now in her arms. He wouldn't open his eyes, and his breathing was shallow. He felt cold, but he wasn't shivering. He didn't have the energy to. "It's not uncommon for a *tikbalang* to make its victims sick, but this . . . I will do what I can, but . . ."

Hiraya couldn't say what she suspected they both knew. There was a chance the boy could recover, but even if he could, she wondered if he'd ever be right again, ever be whole. Something was taken from the boy. Children were resilient, they healed, but even the energy of youth had limits.

"This isn't right," May said. "This isn't what they do. Not normally."

Hiraya glanced back up at May, but it wasn't May who was talking. Not really. It was the black thing, the only being Hiraya knew was older than herself. Even May's tone shifted, having a deep and unnatural reverb. In her entire life, nothing disturbed her as much as her niece, whom she had raised since infancy, sharing her being with the black thing.

"It said something about getting revenge," May said.

"Revenge for what?" Hiraya asked.

"No idea." May looked at the boy. "What the *tikbalang* took. What if I can get it back."

At that moment, Hiraya didn't see the vivisected monster with a mouth full of fangs and fleshy wings. She saw the crying infant her sister left on her doorstep, the little girl who took her first steps into her house, and the young woman who stood up to her when her mother was causing havoc in the village. Hiraya spent centuries never forming ties to places or people. That was, until May. "You can't be seriously thinking of going back out there? The night is growing short, and you know what will happen if you don't revert back to your human form before first light!"

"I have to." May looked at the boy with a long, sorrowful face. "I can't let him die."

"This isn't about the boy . . ."

"Angelo," May interrupted. "His name is Angelo."

"This isn't about Angelo," Hiraya said. "This is about your own guilt. Guilt over what you are, what you had to do in service of the black thing."

"How else can I live with myself," May shouted back, "if I can't find some way to use this curse for good?"

"You already do," Hiraya said. "How many women have you saved? Women who could have died turning to some quack doctor peddling snake oil or risking death from a troubled pregnancy? The women on these streets look up to you. You help them - "

"By killing!" May snapped. "I'm a monster!"

"Only if you chose to be."

May spread out her wings in a woosh. "This is me choosing not to be."

May took to the air before Hiraya could say anything else. Without the boy – without Angelo – May sped off like a bullet into the night. She held Angelo in her arms, but her heart was with her niece. There was nothing she could do now to help May, so she carried Angelo toward her house. She would do whatever she could to keep the boy alive for as long as possible. She didn't know if May would get back in time, if May would have what she needed to save the boy, or if May would return at all. All she could do was try to have hope.

Racing through the night air once again, she headed to where she had left the *tikbalang*. She didn't expect it to still be there - the thing was faster than she was when not injured and could be anywhere by now – but it was the logical place to start searching. She kicked herself – or would have if she still had legs – for not discussing strategy with her *tita* before flying off. She needed a plan, so she turned to the black thing again.

The tikbalang *has Angelo's* . . . Here words failed her, but concepts of a soul or life force formed in her mind. *How do I get it back?*

May wished the black thing would speak in a language instead of vague feelings and concepts, but she understood what the black thing was conveying. *Give up. Not worth it. Dangerous.*

Of course, the black thing wasn't concerned for May's safety. It didn't care about its host so long as it could jump to a new one. She had a clear sensation of the black thing's raw fear of being ripped from May, only to be left on the jungle floor, forgotten and starving for eternity.

Then you better tell me how to beat it, May thought.

There was some hesitation, and May got the sensation of it missing her mother, that May was more trouble than she was worth.

Too bad, May thought. *We're stuck with each other. Now tell me what I need to know!*

After another moment of hesitation, May had her own memories played back to her, that of the *tikbalang* running below her, its black mane flowing except for the three stiff hairs along the spine, so thick they were almost quills. They practically glowed in her memory, like the black thing was highlighting them. She felt a need to pluck them from the *tikbalang's* neck, one sent to her by the black thing. It sent her a clear mental image of her holding the three hairs while the *tikbalang* kneeled obediently in front of her.

I can tame the tikbalang. It wasn't a question but a confirmation. She understood without words what the black thing was telling her. If she plucked the three hairs from the back of the *tikbalang's* head, it would break its will . . . no, that wasn't quite right. She would take its will. It would be an obedient servant. *Then I can order it to return what it took from Angelo.*

Now she just had to find it again.

She reached the spot where she last saw the *Tikbalang*. There was no sign of the horse-faced creature, so she sniffed the air. The thing had been wounded, bleeding. She searched for the coppery smell of blood but caught something else. Tobacco, maybe? Something like burning hair? The black thing inside her stirred as it recognized the scent of the *tikbalang*. Again, the black thing sent May all its fears and misgivings but May ignored them. She banked toward the smell and followed it into the jungle. She had to fly low and slow to not lose the scent, and the black thing screamed in voiceless protest in her mind. Gliding so close to the ground, she was vulnerable.

No choice, she thought.

The black thing disagreed. There was a wave of concepts washing over her - of everyone dying, of equating people to livestock raised for slaughter, of the lives of humans being beneath them – but May shut them out.

I used to be human, May thought to the black thing.

The black thing scoffed at her, shooting her feelings of superiority.

Humans are more than you'll ever be, May thought, *and I'm going to be human again!*

The thought surprised her so hard that it almost knocked her out of the sky. For the first time since the black thing crawled down her throat and turned her into a *manananggal*, she felt hope – no, resolve – that she would be human again. She could feel the black thing inside her shrinking from her mind.

That's right, she thought. *I'm in charge, and nothing will stop me! I'm going to save Angelo, then I'm getting rid of you!*

Large claws ripped through one wing. No longer able to catch the air, she spun and crashed to the ground. Dirt and rocks bit her flesh as she slid across the jungle floor. Before she came to a stop, she felt a hoof stomp on her back and pin her to the ground. Coarse fingers wrapped around the bones of her wings, the claws piercing her flesh as the *tikbalang* tried to rip her wings off her back. May screamed in pain, forcing her body to stay intact, the base of her wings thickening . . .

She was a *manananggal,* an *aswang.* Her body was like clay. She was reshaping her body out of reflex to protect herself, to counter the assault from the *tikbalang,* but she was only limited by her mass and her imagination. Her wings shrunk to half their size as she redirected her flesh toward her back. Twin spikes shot out from her shoulder blades and struck the *tikbalang* in the chest. It howled in pain as May's spikes pierced its flesh, then she forced the ends to grow barbs before pulling the spikes back into her body. The barbed ends ripped chunks of fur-covered meat from the *tikbalang's* chest.

As the *tikbalang* staggered back, she forced her body to mend while scampering away like a bug. She heard the black thing chuckle at her as if to say *who's superior now?* May realized it let the *tikbalang* blindside her. That had its own disturbing connotations, but she would deal with the black thing later. For now, she needed to deal with the *tikbalang.*

The *tikbalang* was on the run again. The copper smell of blood was strong, dominating the scent of tobacco and burnt hair she now associated with the horse-faced monster. Her counterattack had wounded it, costing it a lot of blood, but if she could reshape her body to force it to heal almost instantly, it wasn't unreasonable to think the *tikbalang* could too. She stretched out her wings and flexed them. They were stiff and sore, but she willed them to move. Her body was like clay, and it would obey her will. She flapped and lifted her ripped and torn body into the air. Then she flew after the *tikbalang*, eyeing the three thick hairs she needed to pull.

She climbed higher. The stench of blood was pungent, so she didn't need to be as low, and there was safety in altitude. She was what she hoped was out of the *tikbalang's* reach but not so high she lost the scent. It was fading, though, which made May think it was healing its wounds and traveling faster. She flapped harder, her wings aching in protest. The black thing sent waves of fear through her, letting her know the *tikbalang* was leading them deeper into the jungle and further away from where she rooted her lower half. Every meter into the wilderness was a meter she had to fly out before the sun rose.

Now you care to help, May thought to the black thing. She didn't bother with its reply. She knew it didn't care about her, just its dread over being abandoned and forgotten in the untamed jungle. However self-serving its warning may be, it was still a valid point. May wondered if that was part of some plan of the *tikbalang*. Perhaps it hoped that she would be forced to turn back, or she would be caught by the dawn, and it would let the sun kill her for it. On that thought, the black thing screamed to turn back so forcefully she almost fell from the sky.

No, she said. *I'm not letting Angelo die!*

May spotted the *tikbalang* zigzagging through the trees. She tucked her wings back and let gravity accelerate her, zooming side to side as she dove after it. She could see the three thick hairs bouncing in its mane like it was taunting her. Reaching out with her claw, they dangled just out of reach.

Her body was like clay.

One arm shrunk as her other one elongated. Her arm wobbled as she struggled to control the long pole-like arm against the rushing air. One of the hairs danced in and out of her grip, and every twitch of her arm overcorrected due to the extra length. The *tikbalang* didn't make it any easier, jerking its shoulders to the side to keep them out of her grip. Frustrated, she grabbed whatever she could, her claw gripping a fistful of coarse black hair. The *tikbalang* sprinted, trying to shake her. The arm holding its mane retracted as she reeled herself in, pulling herself closer. As the one arm anchoring her to the *tikbalang* shortened, the other arm grew back to its regular length and reached for one of the hairs.

The *tikbalang* stopped and spun, slashing at May with its claw. Its nails ripped through her chest, forcing her to let go, but before the *tikbalang* could dart away, she lashed out with her veins, her arteries, her intestines . . . any spare part she wasn't using. They wrapped around the *tikbalang* like vines, gripping it tightly. It tried to pull away, swiping at May, but she flew just out of reach, the flesh lashing her to the horse demon pulled tight like kite strings. She reached out with more flesh from her eviscerated abdomen, tangling up his other arm as it attempted another strike. The *tikbalang* struggled against its bonds, but as May held it in place, she took advantage of the distraction. One tendril of her flesh snaked up along its back, curled around one of the quills, and yanked.

The *tikbalang* howled in fury and shock. It twisted and flung its arms wide, cutting its limbs free. May screamed in pain, her intestines and blood vessels flailing, spraying the area with clotted blood and bile. Now cut free, she flew backward out of control but focused less on flying and more on securing the thick hair. Still gripped with a tendril of entrails, she tightened her grip and sucked that tendril back into her body as the *tikbalang* desperately grabbed it. May flapped out of reach, still struggling to right herself, and took the hair in her hand. She climbed until she was at a safe altitude, then leveled herself off.

She looked down at the hair in her hand. It caught the moonlight at certain angles and gleamed with a golden highlight. It was nearly as long as her arm. She quickly braided it into a makeshift bracelet and slipped it onto one wrist. One down, two more to go.

The *tikbalang* was gone again.

May growled to herself. She could find it again, but it would take time. The moon was already low in the sky. She didn't have much time. Gliding closer to the ground, she renewed her search for the *tikbalang*, following its scent. It wasn't far, judging by the pungent strength of tobacco and –

"What do you think you're doing?"

May pulled to a stop and hovered. The grass and leaves under her danced which each flap of her wings. Standing in front of her was her *tita*. "What are you doing here?"

The wrinkled old woman scowled at her. "Looking for you. Foolish child, don't you know how late it is?"

"You're supposed to be caring for Angelo," May said.

Her *tita* waved off her concern. "The boy is stable, but I need the hair to treat him."

She reached out her hand, but May just stared at it. "Why?"

"I found a treatment for the boy, but it requires the hair of the *tikbalang* that attacked him."

Her *tita* stepped forward, her hand still outstretched, but May hesitated. "What do you mean you found a treatment. Where?"

"Does it matter?" her *tita* asked. "You want to argue about it? Or do you want to cure the boy?"

May reached for the bracelet of the *tikbalang's* hair, but she hesitated. Something was off. "How did you get out here so fast?"

"What are you talking about? You haven't gone that far. You two keep going in circles, then stopping to fight. The house is just right over there." She pointed with her chin to the east, finally dropping her hand. May looked over her shoulder but saw nothing but trees. She flapped harder, gaining some altitude, when her *tita* snapped, "What, you don't believe me? I've taken care of you since days after you were born, and this is the thanks I get?"

"How did you find me?"

Tita Hiraya huffed. "You two have been making a racket. All I need is a pair of ears."

Not only did she get a sense that something was off with her *tita's* story, but the black thing felt something as well. May sensed that it knew something and didn't want to say it out of spite. Guarded, she said, "Take me to Angelo, then. Let's get him cured."

"Fine," her *tita* spat. She turned and marched what May was sure was not toward the house but away from it, deeper into the jungle. "Come on, then. Let's get this done since it is so important to you."

"What do you mean by that?" May asked.

Her *tita* looked over her shoulder, not stopping her trek into the jungle. "You think saving one child makes up for all the blood you've spilled?"

May felt like she'd been slapped. "I didn't ask to be like this! This is my mother's fault, you know this! You were there!"

"Oh, whine, whine, whine," her *tita* said. "If you truly felt guilty about what you've done as a *manananggal*, you'd just let it all end."

"What?"

"Just stay out," her *tita* said. "Stay out all night. Let the sun end you. Let your body turn to dust. End it all."

May couldn't believe what she was hearing. She shot in front of her *tita* and hovered before her, stopping her *tita* in her tracks. "You were the one who told me that even a snake had a place in this world! You said you would stick by me, and we would figure it out together!"

"But you don't want to do that, do you?" Though her *tita's* words were kind, there was a threatening and sinister undertone. "You want to end it all, isn't that true? Release yourself from this curse? Escape your guilt? Sunrise isn't too far away. Just stay out a little longer, and the dawn will take care of the rest."

The black thing stirred at that, its self-preservation preventing it from staying silent. It screamed, it threatened, it begged for May to not destroy herself. Amongst those sensations was a question – why did Angelo wander off with the *tikbalang*? Why would Angelo stroll off into the jungle with a two-meter-tall horse demon?

He wouldn't, May thought. *Not unless the monster wasn't a monster.*

"*Tita* Hiraya? Why are you telling me these things?" Her *tita* walked past and continued into the jungle as if she didn't hear May. "*Tita* Hiraya? Answer me!"

Her *tita* looked back, confused, as if she didn't recognize her own name.

May stopped.

Because she doesn't, May thought. *Because in my mind, I still think of her by her real name.*

The *tikbalang* took the form of someone Angelo trusted to lure him away from his home. It now took the form of the only family she had. The only way it could do that was to pull information from her mind. But in her mind, she wasn't Hiraya. Eighteen years of her *tita's* true identity was ingrained in her, so much so that she had to consciously translate her *tita's* name to Hiraya.

May spun, striking out with her wings like a spinning sawblade. There was a fraction of a second, less than an eyeblink, where she second-guessed herself. What if she was wrong? What if this was her *tita*, the woman who raised her since birth?

Her *tita* leaped back, soaring two meters into the air as her body elongated like dough stretched into noodles. Her gnarled and vein-covered hands lengthened to slender and lethal claws, and May heard the snap of her *tita*'s legs as a hock reformed and her toes fused into hooves. Her long grey hair thickened and darkened as it turned back into the lush mane of the *tikbalang*. It slid to a halt on the jungle floor, one front claw digging up the dirt like a plow. It snarled at her, its large square teeth glinting in the moonlight.

"Damn you, *manananggal*!" it spat. "Why does a killer like you fight so hard to save one insignificant human life?"

"No life is insignificant!" she shouted back.

May soared at the *tikbalang*, her hands morphing into lethal talons as she slashed at the horse demon. It zipped backward, locks of fur flying in the air, the only bit of the *tikbalang* her nails had reached. May swung over and over, not giving the *tikbalang* a chance to think, keeping it from countering, but she had to get it to turn around. She needed the two remaining hairs on the back of its neck.

May spun again, stretching out her wings, but this time she extended her wing tips at the last moment. They stretched long and sharp like knives, countering the *tikbalang's* dodge and slicing its cheek. The horse demon howled in pain, staunching the blood with one claw and reflexively spinning away. With the back of its neck exposed, May reached out with her other wing and sliced off one more of the thick hairs. The *tikbalang* tried to turn and reach for it, but he had to fight his own momentum, whereas May had inertia working for her. She got to the hair first. The *tikbalang* must have decided it was a better strategy to protect his last hair because it bolted away instead of fighting back.

Oh, no, you don't, May thought, this time to herself and not the black thing. She took the second hair, took the first off her wrist, and braided the two together into one woven bracelet while climbing back into the air. She slipped the new thicker bracelet back onto her wrist as she looked for the *tikbalang*.

One more, May thought. She was running out of time, though. Dawn wasn't far away. This time, however, it didn't take her long to find the *tikbalang*. It knelt in a clearing. Suspecting a trap, May flew to the edge of the clearing but went no further. Instead, she circled the *tikbalang*, claws extended and waiting for whatever it had planned.

"I surrender," the *tikbalang* said. "I only ask that you kill me instead of taking my last hair."

"Why?" May asked.

The muscles of the horse demon tightened as it held in its emotions inside. "I would rather be dead than a mindless slave."

May cocked her head, pulling from the centuries of knowledge the black thing had collected. "Taking the three hairs tame the *tikbalang-*"

"That's what they call it," it said. "What it means to a *tikbalang* is you lose your free will. You become nothing but a golem, not even able to feed yourself unless your master orders you to." He hissed the word *master* with all the disgust he could muster. "Worse, we stay aware of what is happening, trapped in our bodies. It's a living hell."

The *tikbalang* started heaving, reaching up to its long snout as it coughed up something into its claw. It was ethereal, with whisps of fluorescent blue that danced in the night.

Angelo's essence.

"Try to take it, and I will destroy it," the *tikbalang* said, "and the boy will surely die. Try for the last hair, to try to tame me, and I will destroy it. But if you strike me down, I will release it."

May continued to circle the *tikbalang*. She didn't get a sense it was lying to her, but she couldn't imagine any being so willing to give up its life. "Why should I believe you?"

"I told you why."

"Why throw your life away?"

The *tikbalang* snarled. "It's better than the alternative."

"No, I mean-" May paused, reorganizing her thoughts. "Just give me Angelo's essence, and I'll let you go. You don't need to die."

The *tikbalang* deflated. "I don't care. My life isn't worth preserving."

May inched closer. "All life is worth preserving."

The *tikbalang* snorted. "Says the eater of the unborn."

May growled, but she swallowed her anger. The situation wasn't adding up, and the *tikbalang's* behavior grew more puzzling. "Why did you take Angelo? You said something about revenge. On Angelo? On Tala? What could they have done to you?"

"Why do you care?" The *tikbalang's* head drooped so far that its horse-like head almost touched the ground. "No one cares about me. My own mother cast me off. Ripped me from the womb before I was born and tossed away."

May felt the memories of the black thing seeping into her consciousness, tales of unintended consequences to terminated pregnancies. One such result was the creation of a *tikbalang*.

"For a while, I accepted it," the *tikbalang* said. "I figured my mother never wanted children, that the only thing wrong with me was who conceived me. But then she got pregnant again, and this one she kept. Why?" He slammed his fist into the ground. "Why was Angelo worth keeping when I was not? It wasn't that she didn't want kids. She just didn't want me!"

May drifted toward the *tikbalang*. "Your *nanay* didn't have a choice."

The *tikbalang* shot to his feet and stuck his snout in her face. May ignored the fear pulsating from the black thing and stood her ground. The *tikbalang* screamed, "Of course, she had a choice! She chose to throw me away!"

"No, she didn't," May said. "She told me what happened. She got sick, and the pregnancy went wrong. If she didn't end it, you both would have died. Even given no choice, it was still a heart-wrenching decision for her."

The *tikbalang's* fist-size nostrils flared as it snorted, then turned away. "I wish I could believe that."

"She named you," May said.

The tikbalang stood motionless and silent for a while, then it said, "Is that true?"

"Yes," May said.

"What . . . what did she name me?"

"She said if she had a boy, she would have named it Maliksi," May said.

When the *tikbalang* turned back to her, tears were streaming from its large black eyes. It handed the swirling blue aura to May. "Take it. Return it to the boy."

May reached out to take it, but the black thing howled in desire. It was pure life essence, not as pure as what it extracted from those still in the womb but concentrated, and the black thing wanted to devour it. It ordered May to take it, to absorb it into herself, to feed on that part of Angelo's soul –

"No! Shut up!" May shouted as she jerked her hand away. Slowly, she turned back to the *tikbalang*. "Sorry, not you."

The *tikbalang* withdrew his hand, wrapping its fingers around the dancing blue light in its palm. "Who are you?"

"We don't have time," May said. "We have to get that back to Angelo."

"You want me to trust you," the *tikbalang* said, narrowing its eyes at her. "What are you? When does a *manananggal* care about human lives?"

May let out an exasperated sigh. She could feel the night crawling to an end, but more than that, she could feel the black thing squirming inside her like it wanted to leap out of her and gorge itself on Angelo's essence.

As if it could, May thought, *then my nightmare would be over.*

The *tikbalang* stood motionless, waiting for a reply. May hung her head. "I didn't ask for this. I was a normal human girl once. My mother was getting older. She couldn't carry it much longer."

The *tikbalang* crossed its arms. "I thought *manananggal* were immortal?"

"The black thing is, yes. After centuries, though, my mother's body wore out beyond even its dark magic to keep intact. So, she had me to be the next host for the black thing. I fought them both, but-" May held out her arms to illustrate the inevitable end to her story. "All I want is to be rid of it, to be human again."

"In the meantime," the *tikbalang* said, "the black thing continues to feed."

May hung her head. "A knife can kill, or it can be used to help cure. I try to choose those where taking a life can save a life. If not those, then the unwanted ones. The black thing doesn't always make it easy. It constantly talks to me and feeds me its gluttonous desires. It makes real food taste disgusting, so I won't eat it."

"Why would it do that?" the *tikbalang* asked.

"Because then my human body would die. I will only live off the black thing's power when that happens. Then, I'll never be able to remove it without dying, and its hunger will become mine. It wants me to be dependent on it, so I will be its slave." The *tikbalang* looked at the swirling essence in its hand, and May said, "It has to be you who returns it. It's not safe with me."

Now it was the *tikbalang* who hung his head. "I couldn't. I couldn't face her."

"It would mean so much for her to have her son back," May said. "Both of them."

"She wouldn't want me." The *tikblang* looked down at its claws, still coated with May's dried blood. "Not as I am now."

May fluttered over and laid a hand on the *tikbalang's* shoulder. "Your mother will love you no matter how you are, Maliksi."

Tears pooled from his large, black eyes. "You think so?"

"Yes, I do." She kept to herself how that acceptance would come after the initial shock of seeing her son as a *tikbalang*. She wasn't sure how she would explain it to Tala, but May was confident Talal would accept Maliksi . . . eventually.

Or perhaps she was being naïve.

"We are running out of time," May said. "I need you to take that back to Angelo now."

The *tikbalang* – Maliksi – nodded to the bracelet made from his two braided hairs. "Can I have those back?"

She thought about it, then said, "I'll keep these. For now. Call it insurance."

Maliksi got to his feet. "As you wish."

And then he was gone. For a moment, May wondered if she had made a mistake and if her trust in the *tikbalang* had been misplaced, but the path Maliksi blazed led right back to her *tita* and Angelo. May flew in the same direction as fast as she could.

High in the air, she could see a strip of pale blue on the horizon. Dawn was quickly approaching. She flapped as fast as she could. Underneath, she could see Maliksi racing through the jungle. Inside her torn guts, the black thing was in a panic, its fear adding to her own, the combined fear adding to her speed. The horizon's glow grew brighter, starting to push back the night. She was almost out of time.

She saw it, the stump that was her lower half. She swooped down at it like a hawk after a mouse. At the last moment, she splayed out her wings and came to a rest on top of her lower half. Immediately, the rough bark-like shell started melting away as her body stitched itself back together. All the while, the sky faded from black to dark blue. The black thing slid down into place as the roots sucked back out of the ground. The trunk split, reforming her legs and feet. She stood there, back in her human form, as the first ray of sunlight hit her.

As she dressed, Maliksi came up next to her. She didn't feel self-conscious clothing herself in front of him, perhaps because he wasn't human. She hurried regardless. She needed to see Angelo. Leading Maliksi into the house, he had to duck to clear the doorway.

Angelo lay on a mat, her *tita* crouched over him, dabbing his forehead with a damp cloth. Angelo looked very pale. Every wheezing breath he took was an effort. When her *tita* looked over her shoulder and saw the *tikbalang* filling the room, she shot to her feet. Before either could do anything, May held up her arms and got between them. "It's okay. He's here to help."

Her *tita* didn't look convinced. She locked her eyes on the *tikbalang* but stepped aside and let him approach the boy. She supervised as Maliksi took the swirling essence in his palm and raised it not to Angelo's mouth but his own. He sucked it up into himself, and May absentmindedly started playing with the bracelet of woven hair on her wrist. Then Maliksi bent down and pulled the boy's mouth open. Angelo's eyes popped open wide, fear written all over his face, but with no energy to fight back. Maliksi blew out the blue essence from his mouth and into Angelo's. It funneled down the boy's throat like it was being sucked in, as if it knew where it belonged and was anxious to return home. As more blue aura entered Angelo, his breathing slowed and became less labored, and the color eased back into his complexion. When Maliksi was done, Angelo lay calmly on the mat.

Maliksi caressed the boy's hair, then got to his feet. As he approached the door, May called, "Where are you going?"

"You got what you needed," he said.

"Yes," May said, "and now you can go back to Tala-"

"Stop. I don't blame you, *manananggal*. You said what you needed to in order to save the boy, but I never believed it." He uncurled his long claw. "My hairs, if you please."

May looked down at the bracelet, then glanced back to Maliksi. "You want this back? You need to do one last thing for me."

Maliksi dropped his claw and sighed. "Do I have a choice?"

Tala sat on the old log in the back of her house, a blanket wrapped around her shoulders. She had sat there all night staring out into the jungle, waiting for her son to return, but he never did. May promised she'd find and return him to her, but May never returned. Tala wondered if May was still roaming the jungle looking for Angelo and whoever had taken him. Tears cut clean paths through the dust on her cheeks, but she had cried her eyes dry by dawn.

"*Nanay?*" someone called out. It took Tala a moment to realize the voice belonged to Angelo. It was a hallucination brought on by grief. It had to be, but however logical that explanation seemed, hope brought her to her feet. She couldn't believe her eyes, and fresh tears ran down her cheek. Angelo was running down the street toward her, his arms open wide. Tala almost didn't notice May strolling behind him, her eyes only on her son. She knelt and caught her son as he nearly tackled her, the two throwing their arms around each other.

"I never thought I'd see you again," Tala said, smelling his hair. There was a tinge of tobacco that didn't belong there, but she was too overwhelmed to question it. She looked up at May, who was walking up so gracefully she could be coasting on a cloud. "Thank you."

"It was my pleasure," May said.

Tala grabbed Angelo by his shoulders and held him in front of her. "Why did you wander off?"

"That's something we need to talk about, actually," May said. "There's someone you need to meet."

Tala stared at May in confusion, but May looked out at the untamed jungle. Tala looked over her shoulder in the same direction. At first, she saw nothing but an endless sea of trees. Then there was something – a tree or some kind of animal? – moving amongst the leaves. Before she could make out the form and comprehend what she was looking at, four long, spindly limbs crawled out of the tree line. It hunched over, its long horse-like head hung low to the ground.

Tala didn't scream, but only because the sight of the *tikbalang* froze her in place. The only instinct that overruled her fear was the one to pull Angelo protectively into her arms, but Angelo gently pushed himself free.

"It's okay, *Nanay*," Angelo said. He walked toward the emaciated creature now in her backyard. Tala reached out to catch him, but Angelo walked to the *tikbalang* without fear. Angelo wrapped his hand around one of its long claw-tipped fingers and led it to his mother like a scolded dog. "He's my friend. He wasn't my friend before, but he is now."

"Tala?" May said, stepping forward. "This may be hard to explain-"

But Tala wasn't listening. The *tikbalang* wouldn't meet her gaze as she got to her feet, but something about its eyes called to her. Her heartbeat slowed as she walked over to the giant creature. She caressed its long snout, feeling its course fur, then tilted its head up to her. Then she began to cry anew.

"Maliksi?" she asked.

At first, the *tikbalang* said nothing. Then its own tears started to pool in his large black eyes. "You recognize me?"

Tala nodded, smiling wide. "Of course. I'm your mother."

Maliksi seemed to melt in front of Tala. "I'm sorry. I was angry. I was wrong-"

"Shhhhh," Tala said, stroking his long fur-covered nose. Wet spots darkened his fur as Tala's tears landed on him. "I'm sorry too. But you're here. You've come back to me. That's all that matters."

And the thin and hideous creature felt a mother's love for the first time in its unnatural life.

How many days had passed since the night May rescued Angelo in the jungle? When you were immortal, the days blurred together, but Angelo was still a young boy, so it couldn't have been too long. He was running in circles around his big brother. Maliksi was in his human guise, as was typical for him these days, but May still saw the equestrian features in his face.

Angelo saw May, and his face lit up. Angelo remembered everything from that night. While he still had nightmares of the *manananggal* whisking him into the air, he never connected that eviscerated monster with the beautiful woman standing in the street before him. He was passed out when May handed him to her *tita* Hiraya, and May had returned to her human form when he awoke.

How many days had passed since the night May and Maliksi fought in the jungle for Angelo's soul? The days blurred together when you were immortal, but enough of them had passed for Angelo and Maliksi to bond as the brothers they were. Angelo led Maliksi by the hand, both smiling.

"How are you boys doing?" May asked.

"Maliksi is going to get me *turon*," Angelo said.

"Is he, now?" May said to Angelo, then looked up at Maliksi. "I have something for you."

May slid the bracelet off her wrist and handed it to Maliksi. At first, he stared at it, not daring to believe it. He reached out with a slow and deliberate hand like the bracelet made of his woven hair would turn to smoke if he grabbed it too quickly. Once firmly in his hand, Maliksi smiled. "Are you sure?"

May shrugged. "I trust you. And if you double-cross me, I'll come to take them back."

Maliksi's smile grew wider as he slid it onto his own wrist.

"Thank you."

"It's no problem," May said.

"No, I mean, thank you for everything," Maliksi said, placing one hand on his brother's shoulder.

"It was my pleasure," May said.

She turned to leave when Maliksi called out, "May, wait. I have something for you." He reached into his pocket and pulled out a small berry of a type May didn't recognize. "Eat this, quickly."

"What is it?" May asked. The black thing was emanating apprehension now.

Maliksi moved at lightning speed, popping the berry into her mouth. He clamped her mouth closed and pinched her nose. Like all human food, it tasted horrible, but Maliksi forced her to swallow. When Maliksi let go, May pulled away. She resisted the urge to decapitate the *tikbalang* right there on the street for everyone to see. The powers of the black thing were weaker in the sunlight, but she was far from helpless.

Except that now, she didn't feel the black thing. There was a kind of numbness throughout her body. She stared at Maliksi. "What did you do? What was that?"

"Something I learned from living with other *tikbalang* in the mountains," Maliksi said. "It is a fruit known only to them."

May laid her hand on her stomach, but she felt nothing. She didn't hear the black thing for the first time since becoming May. "What did you do?"

"I put it to sleep," Maliksi said. "Sorry for not telling you what

I was doing, but I had to keep the secret from the black thing. It would try to stop me."

May was beside herself. It was so quiet in her mind now. It was so peaceful. "How long? Is it-"

"Forever?" Maliksi finished her question. "No. Eventually, it will get so hungry it will wake up again no matter how many berries you eat, but until then, you will have some peace. It comes at a cost, however. With the black thing asleep, you won't have access to most of its powers, but you will feel more human." After a pause, he added, "I'm sorry, but that was what you wanted, wasn't it? Or did I misunderstand?"

"No, this is . . . thank you, Maliksi." She leaned forward and kissed his cheek. "Thank you."

"I will gather more if you wish," Maliksi said.

"Yes," May said. "Yes, please."

Maliksi smiled. Angelo tugged impatiently at his arm, pulling him back down the street. May waved them goodbye, then headed back toward her house. She couldn't wait to tell her *tita* the news, but a scent from one of the street vendors pulled her to a stop. Her mouth immediately began to water.

It smelled . . . good.

The street vendor's cart was thin, the sky-blue paint chipped and worn, a single pole in the dead center holding up a patched umbrella to block out the sun. One side was a propane-powered grill. Small white balls of dough were sizzling in a large wok on the grill. The vendor stirred them as they fried in oil, and for the first time since she stopped being human, the scent tingled her nose.

"Would you like some?" the street vendor asked.

May couldn't remember the last time she had fish balls, but she could remember the last time they tasted good, before the black thing sabotaged her taste buds. "I'll take five." she nodded, swallowing down the saliva building up in her mouth.

The street vendor gave a warm smile that showed his missing teeth. "Spicey or sweet sauce?"

"Sweet!" May said, trying and failing to tamp down her excitement.

The street vendor chuckled and spooned the fish balls onto a paper plate. May handed him a handful of pesos and took the sauce-covered balls of dough. She plucked one out with her fingers and popped it into her mouth.

The taste exploded in her mouth. The warm dough, the syrupy sauce, the hint of fried fish mixed with the oil . . . it was as if having them for the first time in her life, which she supposed was kind of true. She closed her eyes as she shut out the rest of the world, letting her sense of taste and smell explore the delicacies in her mouth without distraction.

"Is good, eh?" the street vendor asked.

"Oh, my God, yes," May said, but her elation went far beyond the food she could now eat. May had a thread of hope for the first time in who knew how long. She still needed to figure out how to extract the black thing from her, but she had a weapon in her arsenal for the first time. She had a way of fighting back against the black thing.

I will be human again, May thought.

She expected a rebuttal, to hear the black thing reply in its non-verbal way. For the first time in a long, long time, there was no reply. For the first time since being forced to swallow the black thing, her mind was her own.

May smiled.

ALMOST HOME

The car jostled Rachel awake, and she sat up with a gasp. Her heart raced as she clutched the door handle, unsure what was happening or what to do. With her eyes now wide open, she plucked the earphone out of her ear and looked around. The music blared out of the wireless earpiece until Rachel hit the pause button on the screen of her BEC phone.

"Sorry," her dad said from behind the wheel of the large SUV. "Everything's okay."

From next to Rachel, her baby sister started crying in her car seat. It appeared she was also fast asleep and awoke as scared and confused as Rachel. Her mother twisted around and snaked her body between the two front seats to reach out and caress the baby's cheek.

"It's okay, Ashley," their mother cooed, calming the screaming baby down. Then she turned her head to her husband. "Jim, if you're getting tired, you should pull over. We can get a room-"

"I'm fine," Rachel's father said. "We're only a few hours from home. I just need to stay awake a little bit longer, then I can sleep all I want."

A sense of déjà vu hit Rachel. She twisted in her seat to look behind them. The road they came from was empty save for a single light off the side of a billboard. The rest was nothing but darkness. No pairs of headlights from other cars following them, no red eyes of taillights zooming away on the other side of the dirt median. They were alone.

"Jim, we need to pull over," her mother said.

"Where?" her father asked. "There's nothing out here but desert until we get to San Deigo."

"There has to be a gas station or rest stop somewhere," her mother said. "I need to check the baby, and you need to walk around a bit and wake up."

"I'm fine," her father said. Her mother's silence was more than enough to make her objections clear. "Fine, first place I see to stop, I swear."

"Shhhh," her mother said to the baby, whose wailing had faded to a whimper. "It's okay."

Looking forward again, Rachel looked at the car's info screen in the dashboard's center. "Dad? What's wrong with the map?"

Her father took one hand off the wheel and tried to work the screen, but the car began to drift out of its lane. "Damn it. Grace, can you-"

Her mother let out an exasperated sigh and pulled herself back into the passenger seat. She began pressing buttons on the screen, but the images on the screen flickered and pixilated. "It's not working, Jim."

"Did you try the -"

"I've tried all the buttons."

"You can't just push buttons. You have to know what you are doing."

"I know what I'm doing, Jim," her mother said, a warning sharpness to her voice. "I know how to use the GPS, but it's acting up."

"It's never acted up before."

"Well, I don't know what to tell you because it's acting up now." As she said it, the screen went black except for the white block letters saying *no signal found*. "We must be out of range."

"Out of range?" her father asked. "Of satellites?"

"Well, my cell phone has no service-"

"The car doesn't use the cellular network."

While her parents argued, Rachel took over calming the baby. Ashley's pacifier was tethered to a plastic clip shaped like the head of a smiling teddy bear with a pink bow in its hair. Following the thin pink cord down to where it fastened to the pacifier, Rachel tugged on it until it popped free from where it was wedged between the car seat and Ashley's chubby thigh. Rachel touched the baby's lips with the tip of the pacifier, and Ashley sucked in the teat until the mouth guard was flush against her lips. Rachel offered her finger to Ashley, and the baby wrapped one whole hand around one of Rachel's knuckles. Rachel made a game of trying to pull her finger free, feeling the baby hold on to her with all its minuscule might, as if its life depended on it. It wasn't long, though, before the baby grew tired of the game and let go.

Her parents were still fighting over the GPS, so she pulled up her own phone and loaded the maps app. Typically, the app started with the whole digital globe spinning on her screen, then zooming in on the phone's location, down to the country, then the state, then the point on the city street. This time, however, the globe was a blank black ball, and the app zoomed into nothingness. A blue arrow marked the phone's location on a featureless plane of black.

"Dad, I think something is wrong with the BEC network," Rachel said. "My phone isn't working either."

"Damn BEC," her father growled. "They're too big. That's the problem. They have no competition. No competition means they don't need to bother ensuring their customers are satisfied because where are we going to take our business to?"

"Yes, Dad," Rachel moaned as she slumped back into her seat. Her father had repeated that lecture over and over. She felt she had heard it a hundred times by now.

Her mother patted her father's shoulder, then pointed out the window. "There's a rest stop coming up. Pull over there."

Her father grunted, an odd mixture of annoyance and agreement. "Maybe I can grab a soda, get a little caffeine in me."

"I need a pee," her mother said.

"Thanks for sharing, mom," Rachel said under her breath.

The rest area looked like an oasis of light in the moonless night. Not even the matching rest area on the other side of the freeway could be seen, just the one on their side. The car pulled off the freeway and decelerated rapidly, following the signs for passenger cars as opposed to the roads laid out for the large trailer trucks. Not that it mattered. The rest area was empty of drivers, both civilian and professional. Rachel's father coasted the car into a parking spot and killed the engine.

Rachel climbed out of the car on the same side as her father. After closing the driver's side door, her father clasped his hands together and reached up and back, arcing his spine and stretching out his sore muscles while at the same time pulling his t-shirt up over his flabby belly. His skin was so white Rachel thought he could be a ghost. When he lowered his arms, he wrapped one around Rachel's shoulders, pulling her into a reluctant hug while tugging his shirt back into place over his stomach with the other.

"Ugg, Dad," Rachel groaned. "You smell like death warmed over."

"I am in need of a shower," he admitted. "Few more hours, and we'll be home. Then I can take a three-hour-long shower and sleep for a week."

"In the meantime, do you mind?" Rachel said as she pealed her father's arm off her. From the other side of the car, her mother was carrying the baby and heading to the restrooms, a diaper bag slung over one shoulder. Rachel pleaded to her mother with her eyes, but her mother was too focused on the baby to notice.

"Hey, Princess. What did you think about your brother's school?" her father asked.

Rachel stood on the sidewalk. "What about it?"

Her father shrugged. "I thought it was pretty cool. Your sister loved the dinosaur bones in the science hall."

Rachel rested her arm on one hip. "She was scared of the dinosaur bones in the science hall. She thought it was going to eat her."

"What did you think of it?" her father asked.

"I outgrew dinosaurs a while ago," Rachel said. "I outgrew being called 'Princess' too, by the way."

Her father stepped up and placed a hand on her shoulder. "I mean, what did you think about the campus? The dorms?"

Rachel shrugged. "It's fine, I guess." When her father waited for more, she said, "What do you want me to say? It's a school."

"Just that you're starting high school this year," her father said. "You need to start thinking about college."

"That's, like, years away," Rachel said.

"You need to start preparing now," her father said. "Nick had submitted his applications and was accepted before his senior year started. You only have a couple of years-"

"I haven't even started high school yet, and you have me applying for colleges?" Rachel spat. "God, Dad."

Her dad shrugged. "I don't make the rules. This is how it all works."

"Maybe I don't want to go to college," she said.

"Don't have much of a choice," her father said. "Unless you want to spend the rest of your life living with your mom and dad, working for minimum wage asking your customers if they want fries with their order."

"Okay, whatever," Rachel said. "Doesn't have to be decided tonight, does it?"

Her father ran his hand through his thinning hair. "I don't suppose it does."

Rachel walked up the path to the restrooms and vending machines, a light tan hacienda-style building overlooking the freeway they were just on. The way the buildings were laid out and designed, Rachel was half-expecting to find horse stables. Instead, there were signs for bathrooms on either end. There were no grass lawns to walk on. Instead, the paths were marked off with fences that the government spent a lot of money on to make look rustic. The areas between the walkways were carefully manicured arrangements of desert plants and white rock. The whole place looked like it could have been in a wild west amusement park or museum, if not for the ominous signs warning of rattlesnakes.

Rachel entered the restroom. It gleamed in the bright fluorescent lights, the mosaic tiles creating patterns reminiscent of Native American designs. Everything was polished to a shine, but despite looking clean enough to be the dining room of a restaurant, there was still the stench of stale pee. Across from the sinks, her mother had Ashley on an unfolded plastic changing table bolted to the wall. Her mother looked frazzled, trying to clean the baby while keeping her safely on the table. She looked like she could use another couple of arms.

No sooner had the thought crossed her mind than her mother said, "Rachel, honey? Can you give me a hand, please?"

"Ew, Mom," Rachel said, crinkling her nose. "I told you, I don't do diapers."

"It's okay, it's just a wet one," her mother said. She leaned over Ashley and rubbed her nose with hers. "No stinkies. No stinkies."

Ashley giggled and laughed, kicking her chubby legs. Rachel rolled her eyes but did as she was asked. She took her place beside her mother and held the squirming infant on the table. Her annoyance at being inconvenienced melted at the toothless smile of her baby sister. "Hey, there, goofy-face."

Ashley replied with babbles that made sense only to her. She had the same light-brown hair as Rachel, only a lot less of it. Rachel wished she had the light blond of her mother, but both sisters had a hair color that was a blend of their parents. These days, though, her mother's hair was highlighted with shocks of white.

Her mother dressed the baby, then lifted her off the changing table. "There we go. Does that feel better?"

The baby responded with more cheerful babble. She looked away from their mother and reached for Rachel, who took Ashley's little hand between her thumb and index finger.

"Don't take too long," her mother said as she took Ashley out of the rest area restroom. "We're almost home. Just need to bear with it a little bit longer."

Rachel entered one of the stalls and locked the door. Sitting on the cold but clean plastic toilet seat, she tried her phone while she did her business. None of the apps were working, though. None of the ones requiring an internet connection anyway, though that was most of them. She couldn't pull up any updates on her social media accounts, just all the photos she had taken over the past few days. There were pics of her mom and dad beside Nick, beaming with pride. There was a picture of Ashley in her mother's arms cringing at the fossilized remains of some ancient predator mounted on the wall. Nick's new dorm room, Nick chasing Ashley around the college campus, Nick buying his books for the semester, Nick, Nick, Nick. Rachel slipped her phone in her pocket, finished her business, and left the stall.

Rachel left the row of stalls and turned the corner where a wall of sinks and mirrors waited for her. Washing up in the sink, she splashed the water on her face. It was ice cold and bit her skin, but it woke her up. She brushed her long hair back, light brown except for the streak of pink she added to one side. She shut the water off and reached for a paper towel when a loud bang made her jump. She looked back around the corner to the row of stalls.

"Hello?" she called out. Nobody answered. Did someone else enter the restroom? It was a public place, after all. While they were the only people when they pulled up, maybe another car had visited the rest stop while she was in the stall? "Is anyone there?"

The restroom was quiet. Rachel couldn't even hear her own heartbeat. Right as she blamed it on the wind and turned to leave, she heard it again. The slamming of a stall door being thrown open. Something stepped out of the stall. No, it stepped out of *her* stall, the same one she had used moments before. It was like a living ink blot, vaguely human in shape but featureless. No light was shown on it or bounced off it. It was a mere silhouette of a man. It walked straight out from the stall until it reached the center of the aisle, then froze. Slowly, deliberately, it turned in place until it was facing Rachel.

They stood there facing each other. The silhouette man made no move to attack, didn't wave, didn't even breathe. It just stood there, somehow staring at Rachel with an eyeless face. Rachel was afraid to move, unsure what would break the spell and prompt the silhouette man to come after her. The blood in her veins felt like ice. She swallowed hard and took one slow step backward. The silhouette man didn't move. Clenching her damp hands into fists, she braved another step back. The silhouette man's head tracked her, but otherwise, it remained frozen in its spot between the stalls. Rachel took another step backward, then another, working her way back around the corner and toward the door, leaning forward so her eyes were the last part of her to vanish around the corner. All the while, the silhouette man watched, motionless.

Until it was out of view.

The moment the silhouette man was blocked from her line of sight by the tile-covered walls, she heard footfalls on the floor as the silhouette man walked after her. Rachel didn't wait to see it come around the corner and didn't go back to confirm. She turned and ran as fast as she could, shoving the heavy restroom door out of her way as she came barreling through.

Down the path back to the parking lot, their car was still the only one there. Her father leaned against the hood, sipping a soda as her mother strapped the baby into her car seat. Rachel walked briskly, not wanting to look like she was running but also wanting to get away from the silhouette man as fast as possible. Assuming she didn't imagine it. Assuming she wasn't crazy. She was afraid to look over her shoulder, afraid to see the living silhouette coming after, but just as afraid to see nothing behind her at all.

"There she is," her father sang, his cheery tone at odds with the dread she was feeling. Seeing Rachel in her fast walk, in her not-running run, he cocked an eyebrow. "Everything okay?"

"Yep, all good," she lied as she went past him and opened her car door. "Just anxious to get home."

But her dad was looking back up the way she had come. "Something up there?"

Rachel slammed the car door. "No. No one. Nothing. Let's go."

Her father was still facing the restrooms on top of the hill. He started walking back up the path. "Someone up there? Someone mess with you?"

Rachel threw open the car door and ran back out after her father. She got ahead of him and blocked his path. "No, Dad, really, nothing's up there. I'm just . . ." She swallowed hard. "I'm really tired.

I want to get home and go to bed."

The restrooms tugged at her head like a magnet, but she forced herself not to turn and look. Doing so would be a tell to her father, and she was also terrified of what she might see if she did. Had the thing stayed in the restroom, or did it follow her out? What would her father do if he saw the silhouette man walking down the path? What would she do if she saw it but no one else did?

Her father shifted his gaze from her to the restroom and back again. Rachel could see the gears turning in his head, sensing something was wrong but unable to conceive of his daughter giving him anything but the unvarnished truth. Looking back up at the restrooms, Rachel braved a glance over her shoulder in the same direction. There was nothing up there.

"Okay." Her father began easing back toward the car, but keeping his eyes on the entrance to the restroom. "If you say so, Princess."

"There's nothing there," Rachel reassured him. She didn't consider that a lie. Whatever she saw was made of emptiness.

Once her father was back in the car, Rachel climbed in behind him, though she waited for him to click his seatbelt before pulling her own across her lap. He started the car but sat there with the engine idling, his eyes on the entrance to the restrooms. After what seemed like a century but was, in truth, only a moment, her father put the SUV in reverse. The car rolled back and to the side before stopping, and her father shifted it into drive. As the car moved forward, Rachel looked out the window to the restroom. Standing there in the walkway between the bathrooms was the silhouette man. Rachel snapped her attention forward as if not looking at it would make it disappear. She swallowed down her thundering heartbeat, trying very hard to not look scared. Her father pulled onto the freeway, the only car on the endless stretch of road, and rolled into the night. Rachel turned around in her seat to see the bright lights of the rest area shrink behind them. Even if the silhouette man stood there, they were too far away to see him. Rachel turned back to the front and relaxed in her seat. She rested her head against the cold glass of the car window, watching the blackness outside whiz by as she felt her heart slow. She had no idea what that creature was, but it didn't matter. Real or imaginary, it was behind them now. Soon they would be home, and she could curl up in her own bed and forget she ever saw it.

Rachel didn't know when she nodded off, but the car weaving shook her back awake. She bolted upright, her hand gripping the car door handle.

"Sorry!" her dad called out from behind the wheel. "Everything's okay."

Rachel looked at Ashley, a strong sense of déjà vu hitting her. She expected Ashley to be crying after a rude awakening, but other than a pouting lip and a whimper, she said nothing. Rachel pulled free the pacifier tethered to Ashley from where it was wedged between her thigh and the car seat and placed it in the baby's mouth. Ashley sucked on it lazily, her eyes wide and sad.

"Jim, if you're getting tired, you should pull over," her mother said from the passenger's seat. "We can get a room-"

"I'm fine," Rachel's father said. "We're only a few hours from home. I just need to stay awake a little bit longer, then I can sleep all I want."

"Maybe roll the window down," Rachel suggested as she twisted in her seat. She looked for any hint of the rest area they had left, but all she saw was the base of a billboard, a single light shining back at her.

"Roll the window down?" her father asked.

Rachel spun back around to the front. "Yeah, you know, get some cool air on your face?"

"You'll get the baby sick," her mother said.

"There should be a rest stop where we can pull over," her father said. "I can walk around, maybe grab a soda, get some caffeine in me."

Rachel looked back behind them again. There was no sign of the last rest area. "Again? We just left one."

"They have them every fifty miles or so," her dad said.

"Maybe you should take a nap at the next one," her mother suggested.

"Nah, we're almost home," her father said.

"A half hour won't kill you," her mother said.

A shiver ran down Rachel's spine. She imagined napping in the parked car as the silhouette man walked up the highway after them, right up to the window where she lay unconscious and defenseless. "Maybe Dad's right. We should keep on going."

Ashley began to whimper. Their mother spun around in her

seat to look at the baby. "Aw, you need a diaper change, sweetie?"

Rachel slumped back in her seat and looked out into the unforgiving darkness. There was nothing but black past the dirt and grass-covered median and the opposite lane. She wondered if the silhouette man was out there. In the absolute blackness of the starless night, he could be standing right outside the window, and she wouldn't see him. Maybe the entire length of the road was lined with silhouette men.

In the distance was a faint glow of electric lights. With his hands on the wheel, her father pointed to it with a nod. "Looks like a place to stop up ahead."

As the car pulled off the freeway and rapidly decelerated, Rachel gripped her phone so tightly her knuckles blanched white. She'd gladly trade it for a machine gun, but if she saw the silhouette man again, she could call for help. What she saw, though, pushed all thoughts of the silhouette man out of her mind.

The rest stop was identical to the last one. Not similar. Identical. The Hispanic-inspired architecture, the eaves that reminded her of a ranch house and horse stables, even how it looked new and unmarred by graffiti. It was the same rest stop.

Her father coasted the car into a parking spot in front of the path that led up the hill where the restrooms and vending machines stood. Her parents opened their car doors and hopped out, then her mother opened the rear passenger door and began unbuckling Ashley from her car seat. Ashley seemed uninterested, sticking her lower lip out but not even mustering the energy to cry, though her mother didn't seem to notice. Rachel watched from her seat as her parents walked up the path to the vending machines, chatting and laughing together. She stayed behind, her eyes scanning the area for any signs of danger. She didn't see any hint of the silhouette man, but she couldn't shake the feeling it was lurking out there, hidden in the shadows.

Rachel tried to push the thoughts out of her mind and join her family, but her feet felt like lead, and she couldn't bring herself to move. She watched her father wrap an arm around her mother as her mother laid her head on his shoulder. Still, she couldn't shake the feeling that something was watching her, waiting for its moment to strike. Rachel shook her head, trying to clear her thoughts. She knew it was silly, that this couldn't be the same rest stop, and the silhouette man had to be miles away. Still, she couldn't shake the feeling of unease. She decided to stay near her family and keep watch, ready to protect them if anything happened. She pushed open her door and hopped out, running up the path after them.

Her father stopped at the vending machines, using his credit card to order himself a soda as her mother continued to the restrooms. Rachel heard the heavy soda-filed plastic bottle thud behind her as she turned into the women's restroom. For one heart-wrenching moment, Rachel didn't see her mother or baby sister, only to find her mother bent over the changing table.

Her mother glanced up at her. "Oh, good, you're here. Help me with your sister."

Rachel peered around the corner at the row of stalls. She took a deep breath, forcing her racing heart back down into her chest where it belonged. Approaching the first stall, she raised a shaking hand to the door. For a moment, she froze, her resolve evaporating, but she had to know. If the silhouette man was behind the door, ignoring him wouldn't save her. A little whimper squeezed out from her quivering lips, her nostrils flaring as she breathed harder and harder. She shoved the first stall door open with a bang and jumped back, but it was empty. Turning around, she threw open the next stall door, convinced the silhouette man was standing behind it, but it was also empty. She went to the next stall, and then the next, her heart thundering harder each time, convinced that the next stall door was the one the silhouette man was standing behind. Each time, however, the stall was empty. Her heart didn't stop racing until she shoved open the last stall door.

"If you're done?" her mother called out.

Rachel backed out of the row of stalls, not trusting the silhouette man not to materialize out of thin air. She bumped into the plastic changing table, where Ashley was strapped to it to keep her from rolling off and falling to the floor. Not that she needed to be buckled in. Ashley lay motionless except for her eyes, which looked pleadingly up at Rachel. Her mother handed Rachel the dirty diaper.

"Don't worry, it's just a wet one," her mother said. She leaned over Ashley and rubbed her nose with hers, just like the last time at the previous rest stop. "No stinkies. No stinkies."

But Ashley didn't laugh as Rachel expected. Her mother looked a bit confused as well. As her mother unbuckled her from the changing table, she said, "Someone must be tired."

Ashley didn't look tired to Rachel. She was moving like a toy with the batteries running down, though her eyes looked alert. Sad, but far from sleepy. Ashley looked up at her sister pleadingly, but that had to be Rachel's imagination. What could an infant be asking for?

Her mother pulled Ashley into her arms and folded up the changing table. Together they left the bathroom, leaving Rachel alone. She walked up to the sink and sprayed her face with cold water. She looked at herself in the mirror, the beading water running down her smooth skin. She ran her fingers through the long pink streak she had dyed in her hair.

"Ouch!" she cried, yanking her hand away. Glancing down at her fingers, tiny droplets of blood beaded up on the surface. "What in the world?"

She brought her fingers slowly to her hair again. With a careful and light touch, she parted the strands of hair to find something hard and sharp. Gently, she picked out whatever it was out of her hair and looked at it. Pinched between her thumb and index finger was a thick piece of glass. The ends pressed against her fingers were flat and smooth, but the other sides were faceted, jagged edges. She dropped it in the sink and carefully pulled several more pieces out of her hair.

"Where did all this-?" she started to say when she heard a bang from the stalls. Her heart dropped into her stomach like a rock. Frozen in place, she gripped the sink, her arms quivering. She tried to force herself to move, but the only thing that happened was her breathing became more rapid and shallow. It was like someone was holding her head in place, keeping her from turning to see if the silhouette man was walking around the corner. Finally, she managed a step, and her leg wobbled as if she had just ran a marathon. Leaning on the rows of sinks for support, she side-stepped to the corner and leaned over.

The row of stalls where empty.

With all the fear and adrenaline leaving her at once, she almost collapsed to the floor. She leaned against the wall. The tiles felt cool against her skin as her breathing and her heart rate slowed. When she felt strong enough to leave, her legs still felt like rubber, but she didn't feel like they would give out on her. With careful steps, she walked out of the empty restroom.

Her father was at the vending machines in the middle of the walkway bridging the men's and women's restrooms. Rachel found the bright glow of the machines reassuring. Her father leaned against one of them and sipped a soda before looking at Rachel. "Hey, Princess. How you holding up?"

"I'm fine." She didn't have the strength to complain about him calling her "Princess" again. Instead, she leaned against the vending machines next to her father. She started to relax when her father's hand clasping her shoulder snapped her back awake. She caught herself before she jumped, though her eyes still snapped open.

"Don't worry," her father said, not noticing how edgy his daughter was. "We'll be home in a few hours."

"Yeah," she said. "Home."

"Say, what did you think about your brother's college?" her dad said.

Rachel blinked, then looked up at her father. "What?"

"The college," her dad said. "What did you think of it?"

Rachel crinkled her brow. "You asked me that already."

Now it was her father's turn to blink like he was waking up from dozing off. "Did I?"

"Yeah," Rachel said. "At the last stop."

"Oh." Her dad's face was blank, resembling a computer with too many apps open at once and grinding to a halt. "What did you say then?"

"Not much," Rachel said.

Her father took a deep, readying breath like he was about to defuse a bomb. "Rachel, it's important that we start planning for your future education now. You don't want to be behind your peers when it comes to applying to colleges."

Rachel rolled her eyes to the starless sky. "I'm just starting high school, and you already have me leaving for college."

"The next three years are going to set you up for college," her father said.

"And then I can abandon Ashley the way Nick . . ."

Rachel bit her sarcasm back and looked away, putting the cork back on the bottle of emotions she had been carrying. Her father's hand rested on her shoulder. "Rachel, your brother is still part of this family."

Rachel shrugged her father's hand off. "He left."

"I understand how you feel. I miss him too, but your brother didn't abandon us. He's starting a new chapter of his life. Someday you will start that same chapter, and when you do, we'll support you every step of the way, just like we did for Nick."

She wouldn't meet her father's gaze. If she did, her father might see all the emotions she was wrestling with, the ones she was fighting to keep from escaping. She stormed off back toward the car. "Whatever. Can we go home now?"

Marching back to the SUV, she couldn't understand why she was the only one upset by Nick leaving. Sure, her mother cried when they said goodbye, but it was like Nick never existed once they got back on the road. Why was she the only one missing her brother? Why was she the only one angry at him for leaving? She yanked open her door, climbed in, and slammed the door shut. The other rear door was open, her mother frozen in the middle of buckling up Ashley in her car seat, her eyes now on Rachel.

"Everything okay?" her mother asked.

"Fine," Rachel spat. "Can we go?"

Her mother said nothing. She buckled Ashley in her seat, kissed the baby on her forehead, and closed the door. When the front doors didn't open like Rachel expected, she glanced up to see her parents talking in front of the car. She strained to hear them but could make out the gist of what they were saying. They were talking about her and talking about Nick. Rachel let out a long, exasperated sigh the way only a fourteen-year-old girl can.

Her mother wrapped her arms around herself, hugging herself for warmth against the cold desert air. When Rachel first learned of their trek through the desert, she thought of a scorching hot and dry place, but she never realized how biting cold that same desert could be at night. She almost yearned for the blazing hot sun and the triple-digit temperatures of the day. How many hours until dawn, she wondered. It couldn't be that much longer. It felt like it had been night forever. For that matter, the desert night was getting colder. Her breath came out in a white fog. She wished her parents would get back in the car and start the engine, if for nothing else than to run the heater.

She looked out through the front windshield at her parents, hoping to see them coming back into the car. Instead, she saw a shadow move along the top of the hill by the vending machines. No, not a shadow. Him. The silhouette man. The ache in her lungs reminded her to take a breath, and she gasped for air. Every bead of sweat on her brow felt like a tiny ice cube in the cold night air. Through the fogging windshield, she saw the total blackness of the silhouette man strolling down the path toward her parents.

Her mother and father were too busy talking to each other to see it. A thought hit her, chilling her bones. What if they couldn't see the silhouette man? What if only she could see it? What if it wasn't really there, if he was nothing but a hallucination? She wasn't sure which was scarier, the dark and featureless thing walking toward her unsuspecting parents or that she might be going crazy. She sat frozen. She wanted to warn her parents, but what if that just proved the silhouette man was a figment of her imagination?

Her paralysis was broken when her father turned back to the rest stop buildings. He did a doubletake when he spotted the silhouette man, and a strange mix of relief and dread washed over her. She wasn't insane, but that meant the threat was real, and it was heading their way. Now her mother was looking at it, their previous conversation forgotten. Then, to Rachel's horror, her father started toward the unknown figure.

Rachel popped open the car door. Standing on the door frame, she looked over the roof of the SUV at her parents. "Dad! No! We need to go! Now!"

Her father paused, looking from Rachel to the silhouette man. Her mother put a hand on her father's arm. "Jim, what is that?"

The silhouette man continued down the path without any urgency, as if it expected its victims to wait for him. Her mother clutched at her chest with one hand and wrapped her other arm around her father's upper arm like it was a pole in a hurricane. Her father cocked his head, more puzzled than scared by what he saw, which in Rachel's opinion, was the wrong emotion.

"Dad!" Rachel shouted. "It's coming! We need to go!"

Her father looked from Rachel to the silhouette man, deciding whether confrontation or running was the best plan. Wait too long, and the decision would be made for him. He must have decided that driving away was the best way to protect his wife and two daughters because he sent her mother to the car as he jogged to the driver's seat. Rachel dropped back into her seat, yanked the door closed, and grabbed her seatbelt. Sliding the buckle into its slot was difficult as Rachel's hands wouldn't stop shaking, but she managed. As her father fished out his keys, the silhouette man continued its gradual pace right toward them. Rachel feared her father had lost his keys or would drop them on the floor, giving the silhouette man precious seconds to get closer, but her father put the keys in the ignition without effort. As he turned the key, Rachel was sure all she would hear would be the starter straining to turn the engine over, whining as the battery bled power, but the horror movie cliché didn't happen. The engine started as reliably as ever. Her father turned on the headlights, but while the rest stop was illuminated with the SUV's powerful high beams, the silhouette man remained a block-out matte of pure black.

"Jim! Go!" her mother shouted.

Her father shifted the car in reverse and let the car roll straight back, keeping the lights on the man that light couldn't touch. He sat there for a moment despite the screams from Rachel and her mother. The silhouette man stepped off the curb and walked through the parking space they sat in moments before. Then her father threw the SUV into drive and stepped on the gas. There was no squealing of tires, but Rachel was pushed back into her seat as the car turned and accelerated. They passed the silhouette man on the passenger side. As Rachel watched him as they drove by, she noticed Ashley reaching out to him with one pudgy hand, her tiny fingers opening and closing as if trying to grab him.

Rachel was thrown against the car door as her father took the turn onto the onramp a bit too fast. Once on the straightaway, the engine roared as it raced onto the empty freeway. Rachel twisted in her seat and watched the rest stop fade away into the night.

"Jim, what was that thing?" her mom asked.

"I don't know," he replied. Rachel could hear the material padding the steering wheel creaking under her father's grip. "It doesn't matter. It's behind us now. We'll be safe at home soon."

"It's following us," Rachel said. "I saw it at the last rest stop."

Her parents turned to look at Rachel, though her father turned back to face the road. His eyes flickered between the road and looking at Rachel through the rearview mirror. Her mother reached out between the front seats and took Rachel's hand. "Why didn't you say something, honey?"

"I . . . I wasn't sure it was real," she said. "I thought maybe I was imagining it."

She told them about her first time meeting the silhouette man, how he came out of the bathroom stall and walked toward her, and how she ran. Afterward, her father asked, "Was that all he did? Just walk toward you?"

"Yeah," Rachel said, wrapping her arms around herself. Her dad didn't get how creepy the thing was.

Her dad pressed the microphone icon on the car's touch screen. "Call 9-1-1."

"I'm sorry," a computer voice replied through the car's speakers. "I'm having difficulty understanding you right now."

Her father cursed under his breath and fished his phone out of his pocket. With one hand on the wheel, her father unlocked the phone and dialed 9-1-1. Instead of hearing the call ringing through the car's speaker system, they heard three tones, followed by a pre-recorded message. "We're sorry, your call cannot be completed as dialed. Please hang up and try again."

Her father did just that, the SUV weaving on the road as her father manipulated the phone with one hand. Her mother looked at her father while biting her lower lip as if to clamp her mouth shut and prevent her concerns from finding a voice. Rachel was less worried. There weren't other cars on the road for him to hit. For his troubles, all they got was the same pre-recorded message.

"Looks like we're in a cellular dead zone," her father said, dropping the useless phone into the center console. "We'll pull over at the next gas station or whatever and find a landline."

"When was the last time we saw a gas station?" Rachel asked.

"I'm sure we'll hit one soon," her father said. "We're okay on gas, though, so no worries there."

Rachel leaned back in her seat, scowling. That wasn't really an answer to her question, but she let it go. She rested her head against the cold window and looked out at the inky black night. She didn't know when she fell asleep but was jolted awake when the car wobbled on the road.

"Sorry," her dad said from behind the wheel of the large SUV. "Everything's okay."

"Again?" Rachel asked.

Her mother glanced over at her father. "Jim, we should pull over."

"I know, I know," her father said. "First chance I get. We need to find a pay phone."

"A what?" Rachel asked.

Her father chuckled. "Before everyone had a phone in their pocket, you had to put a quarter in a phone the size of a toolbox mounted on the wall."

"Do they still have payphones?" her mother asked.

"At rest areas? Sure," her father said. "Whether they still work, that I don't know."

"Looks like we're coming up on a rest stop now," her mother said. Was it Rachel's imagination, or were her mother's words dripping with dread?

Rachel sat up and peered through the windshield at the upcoming offramp to the rest stop. "Dad, keep going."

"What?"

"Don't stop here," she said. "Please. Let's find something like a gas station or a diner or something. Some place with people."

"There might be people-" her father started to say.

"We're the only car on the road," Rachel said. "There's not going to be anyone there. Just please, keep going."

"Okay, okay," her father said. "We'll skip this one."

The SUV passed the offramp. Rachel turned in her seat to eye the rest stop as they soared past. Was it the same rest stop as before? It was impossible to tell. If it was the same one, she hadn't seen it from the road, and from that distance, there wasn't a lot of detail she could make out anyway. Still, she had a sinking feeling it was the same rest stop. Not a copy, but the exact same one, like they were in some kind of loop. It was a crazy, irrational idea, one her logical mind dismissed, but the idea festered in her gut like an ulcer all the same. As she watched the rest area go by, she noticed Ashley reaching out with one hand toward the oasis of light. She twisted as much as her car seat would allow to keep the rest stop in sight.

Rachel leaned back against the cool window. With the crisis averted, she allowed herself to relax. She told herself they would reach a gas station eventually. They were miles from the rest stop where they left the silhouette man behind. It wasn't the same rest stop. It couldn't be. Soon they would be home. Soon they would be-

The car jerked back and forth, jolting Rachel awake. When had she fallen asleep again? How long had she slept this time?

"Sorry," her father said.

"Jim, for Pete's sake," her mother said.

"I know, I know," he said. "I'll pull over next chance I get."

Rachel looked over at Ashley to find the baby was staring at her first, as if waiting for her. Ashley looked resigned, a look Rachel didn't think an infant was capable of. "You okay, goofy-face?"

Her mother twisted around in her seat, the seatbelt sliding over her body as it held her in place. "She okay?"

"Yeah," Rachel said. "Just . . . I don't know. Melancholy?"

"Nice ten-cent word there, Princess," her father said, earning him an eye roll from his daughter.

Her mother ignored him and caressed Ashley's cheek. Ashely didn't smile or babble. Her mother studied the baby, not finding anything wrong but seeing the same thing Rachel did. "She's probably just tired. It's been a long trip." Her tone told Rachel her mother was trying to convince herself of this, she was failing to convince anyone, and she knew it. She glanced at her husband. "Can we pull over soon?"

Her father flitted his eyes to her, then back to the empty road. "Everything okay?"

"Yeah, I just want to check the baby," she replied. Her father pulled his eyes off the road to give her mother another look. The two did that married people thing where they talked with their eyes like they were transmitting data over a private Wi-Fi built in their heads. Rachel looked up to the roof of the car and huffed. Most days she was glad she wasn't connected to that network, but she wished she was tonight.

The bright lights glowed on the horizon. Rachel dared to hope it was a gas station, a diner, maybe even a roadside motel, but a rock formed in her gut as she dreaded what she would see. As they drew closer, she saw the same hacienda-inspired buildings at the rest stop. She gripped the handle of the car door, and for a fleeting moment, she thought of throwing open the door and jumping out. But if she didn't kill herself in the fall, where would she go? She was safer in the car than anywhere else, though that wasn't much comfort.

Her dad coasted the car into the parking spot in front of the path that led up the hill to where the restrooms and vending machines sat, which were so brightly lit it looked like the inside of a shopping mall. Despite every inch of the rest stop being illuminated, to Rachel, it looked more ominous than any haunted house. Her dad threw the car into park, and everyone got out of the car as if everything was normal. No, not everyone. Her mother left the car a bit hesitantly, her eyes locked on the restrooms on top of the hill even as she fished Ashley out of her seat.

"Dad, maybe we shouldn't go up there," Rachel said.

Her father stopped and glanced up at the restrooms. "What?"

"You can't see it?" Rachel asked. "It's the same rest stop!

We've come here over and over!"

He looked up at the restrooms, then back to Rachel. "That's silly. We've been driving for hours."

She marched up to him, pointing at the buildings. "It's the same hill, the same restrooms, the same vending machines-"

"Hey!" Her father took her by the shoulders. "Calm down. It's okay. It's not the same rest stop."

"Dad, it is!" Rachel said.

"No, it isn't." Her father looked over her shoulder toward the building on the hill. "It can't be." His words were absent any confidence, but when he turned back to Rachel, all skepticism evaporated. "They probably just look the same because the government hired one company to build them all. They reused the same design, bought the materials from the same suppliers, that kind of thing."

"Dad, it's not like the other rest stops," she said. "It's the exact same one. We've been driving in circles."

"That's not possible," her father said. "We've been on the same highway, going in one direction. This can't be the same rest stop, but I do need to find a phone. We have to call about that . . . whatever that was at the other rest stop. We have to let the cops know."

Before Rachel could say anything else, her father was headed back up the path to the restrooms and vending machines. She stood there, looking at the buildings. Could her father be right? Could all the rest stops be out of a cookie-cutter pattern? She thought about the other rest stops they had visited on their way to and from her brother's college. Sure, they were all similar, but she couldn't remember any two rest stops being identical. Then again, all those other rest stops were visited during the day. Maybe the night was tricking her.

Standing by the car, she noticed her mother frozen in place on the other side, Ashley in her arms. Even the baby seemed still. She forced a weak smile. "C'mon. You can help me change Ashley."

Neither of them moved. Her mother swallowed her fear and forced herself to walk to the restrooms. Rachel went slack-jawed, then her shoulders slumped. Was her mother sinking back into the same denial her father was swimming in? Dropping her chin to her chest, she followed her mother up the path.

Her father was fighting with the pay phone in the area between the men's and women's restrooms, adjacent to the vending machines. It looked both new and antiquated at the same time, like it had just rolled off the assembly line and traveled through time to get installed here and now. Her father slammed the receiver back on the hook.

"Must be on the fritz," her father said as she walked by. "Getting some kind of crosstalk or something."

Rachel entered the gleaming and clean bathroom. She didn't have to search for her mother and Ashley. They were at the changing table bolted to the wall, just like the last time, and the time before that. While her mother's location was predictable to Rachel, her entrance took her mother by surprise. "Oh, good, you're here. Help me change your sister's diaper."

Rachel didn't protest. There was no point. She felt like she was stuck in a Tik-Tok video, repeating over and over. She looked down at her baby sister strapped down on the plastic table. "You okay there, goofy-face?"

Ashley didn't laugh. She didn't smile or babble. Ashley simply lay on the table as if patiently waiting for the big people to finish. She paid their mother no attention as the diaper was peeled open.

"You haven't said much since leaving your brother's college," her mother said as she wiped the baby clean, the words coming out in a slight shiver.

"You want to talk about this now?" Rachel craned her neck to make sure they were still alone.

"Takes my mind off of . . . whatever we saw at the last rest stop." Her mother forced a smile. "Besides, we're safe. We left that thing several stops ago. It's miles away."

Rachel didn't share her mother's optimism. She wasn't sure they were miles away. She started to think they weren't feet away from where she last saw the silhouette man.

"So, you want to talk about Nick?" her mother asked.

Rachel shrugged but kept her eyes on Ashley. The baby, for her part, looked up at her big sister without judgment. "What's to say. He left."

"He didn't leave," her mother said. When Rachel side-eyed her, she rocked her head back and forth. "Well, okay, he left for college, but he didn't leave the family. He didn't leave us."

"Feels like he's not here." Rachel was unable to keep all the sarcasm out of her voice.

"When you have kids, you'll understand," her mother said as

she fastened the new diaper onto Ashley. "It's a natural part of life. Your kids grow up. They move on to have their own lives and their own families. It won't be too long before you move out yourself."

"You're trying to get rid of me?" Rachel smirked.

"No, but it will be only a few years before you finish high school and are off to college yourself." Her mother reached down, unbuckled the now clean and redressed Ashley, and picked her up into her arms. "At least I'll have this little one for a long while."

Her mother rubbed her nose against Ashley's, but the baby looked bored and uninterested. Her mother didn't seem to be bothered by it. She took Ashley and headed out of the bathroom, but at the door frame, she stopped. She looked back past Rachel to the restroom. Rachel knew she was looking for the silhouette man.

"You coming?" she asked.

"In a minute," Rachel replied.

Her mother hesitated, scanning the room but finding no one who wasn't supposed to be there. "Okay. Don't take too long."

She left with Ashley, leaving Rachel alone in the room. She walked over to the sinks and gripped the counter, bending over, staring at the floor. "What the hell is happening to us?"

Leaning back a bit, she spotted something gleaming in the bottom of the sink. Cocking her head to the side, she reached down and gently picked up something small, hard, and sharp. It was clear but coated with wet, sticky blood.

It was the glass. The glass she pulled from her hair at the last rest stop. Except it wasn't the last rest stop. It was this one, the same one.

Rachel looked up at the mirror. Her hair draped down over her head, brown except for the streak she dyed pink. Only now, it wasn't pink. It was dark red, coagulated blood coating it. Her skin was split open at her hairline, exposing her blood-tinged skull.

Rachel screamed, her gaze locked onto her bloody reflection. Only the sound of running footsteps coming behind her pulled her attention away. She turned to see her father skidding to a halt on the polished tile. With manic eyes, he looked around for any threats but found nothing. "What? What is it?"

Rachel stared wide-eyed at her father, her hand raised to the gash on her head but not feeling the sticky wetness of the blood she expected. She turned back to the mirror to find the gash on her forehead and the blood were gone. She snapped her gaze back to her father, who stood there panicked and confused.

"Nothing," she said. "I thought I saw . . . I don't know. My eyes must be playing tricks on me."

Her father took a huge, calming breath. "Okay, let's get going. Let's get out of here."

Her father wrapped a protective arm around Rachel's shoulder and guided her out of the bathroom. She laid her head against her father's chest and felt his strong arm squeeze her as if trying to dampen her shivering. They walked past the vending machines and the pay phone. Halfway up the path stood her mother, stuck between her twin responsibilities. Ashley was nowhere in sight, but the car's rear passenger door was open, sitting under the warm glow of the streetlights. Rachel figured the baby was safely buckled in her seat, and the door left opened so the baby wouldn't be scared or alone. Beyond the reach of the streetlight was the pure blackness of the starless night.

Then part of that blackness shifted. It moved into the glow of the lamps, but the light refused to touch it like oil sliding across the surface of a pond.

The silhouette man.

"Mom!" Rachel screamed, pointing at it.

Her mother turned to see it walking toward them, but instead of running away, she darted toward it. Rachel's heart thundered in her chest, and for a split second, she didn't understand why, but then a shiver of dread and comprehension washed over her.

The silhouette man was bending through the open car door. Her mother was running down the path screaming, but the silhouette man either couldn't hear or didn't care. It stood up, holding Ashley with arms of night. Ashley didn't cry. She didn't even look sad. She reached out to the silhouette man, her pudgy fingers opening and closing. The silhouette man held her to his chest, and she sank into him. As Ashley vanished into the silhouette man, Rachel saw her baby sister turn to her for one last look. The baby was smiling. Then she was gone.

Her mother wasn't screaming. She was shrieking. Fury and grief and anguish and raw anger all flew out of her as she charged at the silhouette man, no longer rational or thinking of the danger. Her hands were curled into claws, and Rachel didn't think it was a figure of speech to say her mother was going to claw Ashley out of the silhouette man, but the man of darkness didn't give her a chance. Like a hole in the universe, the silhouette man was sucked into himself. Before her mother could reach him, the silhouette man was gone.

Her mother fell to her knees and wailed. Rachel walked up to her and knelt by her, putting her arms around her mother, but she had no tears. She felt too numb. Her father charged into the night after the silhouette man, after Ashley, but neither was there.

"Mom, I . . ." Rachel started, but what could be said? What words could help? Ashley was gone.

Her father huffed his way back to the car. "C'mon, we need to go."

Her mother sat unmoving, but Rachel looked up to her father. "What about Ashley?"

Her father was hooking his hands under her mother's arms and getting her to her feet. "We need to find a working phone and call for help. Get the state police, close the highways before whoever took Ashley gets away."

"They're gone," Rachel said. "They disappeared right in front of us. They vanished."

"They can't have. That's not possible," he said to Rachel. Then he looked at her mother. "We'll find her. We'll get her back."

Rachel opened her mouth to protest, but what was the point? To remove any hope from her parents that Ashley could be found? She shut her mouth and helped her mother into the car, her sleeve soaked with her mother's tears. Her father pulled the seatbelt over her mother and clicked it into place. Then he cupped her face and aimed her dead-eye glare at him.

"We'll get her back." He spoke in a soft but confident tone. "I won't stop until we get her back."

Her mother didn't say anything. She didn't nod. Her inhales came in studders as she clutched her chest. Rachel slid into her seat, her eyes going from her mother to the empty car seat beside her. Ashley was so small, but her absence was so huge. As her father backed the car up, Rachel looked around the rest area for the silhouette man and Ashley. It was strange how she ran from him moments ago, but now she'd give anything to find him. As the car pulled away, they left not only the rest stop but any hope of finding her baby sister again. For the first time, the tears started to roll down her cheeks. She leaned against the cold glass of the car window as her tears blurred the world.

The car jolted side to side, shaking her awake. She was surprised, not by the wobbling of the car but because she didn't remember falling asleep. The car jerking back and forth was as predictable as her father's words.

"Sorry," her dad said from behind the wheel of the large SUV. "Everything's okay."

This time, though, her mother didn't speak up to admonish her father for driving tired. There were no suggestions to pull over for a nap or to find a hotel. There wasn't even a sob from her mother. There was just . . . nothing.

Her father reached over and patted her leg. "First chance we get, we'll pull over and find a working phone. We'll call the police. We'll find Ashley."

"There'll be a rest stop coming up in a minute." Rachel twisted in her seat to look out the rear window. The only thing behind them was a single light gleaming at them from the side of the thick metal column holding up a billboard. There was a hint of something in her mind, like a picture that was just beginning to come into focus but still had a long way to go before the subject was recognizable, but she didn't have the heart to put any energy into it.

"There's a rest stop," her father said. "They should have a pay phone. We can call for help."

Her mother still said nothing. She was curled up in her seat, looking like Ashley as she slept. The SUV pulled off the freeway and decelerated. Rachel wasn't at all surprised to see the same Mexican-inspired buildings of the rest stop. She wasn't sure why – though she had a vague idea – they were circling back to the same rest stop, but she was certain now. It was the same one. Not similar, not a copy, but the exact same one.

And he would be here. The silhouette man. The only question she had was, what would he do this time?

Her father threw the car into park and killed the engine. "I'm going to try the phone."

Rachel watched her father hop out of the car, closing the door behind him, and then trot up the path toward the pay phone that she knew wouldn't work any better this time than it had before. The car was swallowed by a stifling silence. Rachel struggled to find words – any words – that could help, working her mouth as if she could cough them up like a cat with a hairball.

"I'm sorry," she said, unsure what she was apologizing for.

The silence crept back in, threatening to suffocate her, when her mother said, "It's not your fault."

Rachel sniffed and rubbed her nose. Her mother was past tears, though. Her grief collapsed in on itself, forming a black hole swallowing every other emotion. Rachel wanted to reach out to her mother to give her some tiny touch of comfort, but she was afraid of being sucked in. "I should have said something when I first saw him, but I thought I might have . . . I don't know, been hallucinating or something?"

She expected her mother to console her, maybe lash out and yell at her, but there was nothing.

"Mom, please be okay," Rachel said. "I need you."

Her mother started shaking her head, but it was how she did that sent a chill down Rachel's spine. There was an odd jitteriness to her slow yet somehow still manic way her head moved, like a short-circuiting robot. "You don't need me. Your brother doesn't need me."

"Mom, don't say that," Rachel said. "Of course I do."

"It's okay," she said, though her voice was devoid of feeling. "You're not supposed to need me. It means I raised you right. It means you're on your way to being a self-reliant young woman. But it also means my job is done. I'm not needed anymore. But Ashley needed me. Ashley . . . Ashley . . ."

It would have been way less terrifying if her mother had crumpled into a blubbering mess, but instead, she was empty. Soulless. Dead inside. Rachel pulled back, curling into the corner of the car.

"Hey, I'm going to check on Dad, okay?"

Her mother didn't reply. Rachel opened the door and slipped out. She felt guilty leaving her mother in the car but even more guilty for feeling relieved to be away from her. She couldn't hear her mother from outside the car, but she could see her mother's lips mouth "Ashley" over and over. Her mother rocked back and forth in her seat, holding her hands to her chest. She almost went back inside despite how uneasy her mother made her, but she heard the distant slamming of the phone back onto its cradle. She looked up the hill to see her father fighting with the pay phone. Giving her mother one last look, she headed up the path after her father.

Her father held his head in his hands as he leaned against the wall and slumped to the ground. Rachel walked up and knelt in front of him. He didn't look from his hands. "I have to find her. I have to get us home."

"Dad, I don't think-"

Her father's expression cut Rachel off as he lowered his hands and looked up. She had never seen a look like that on her father, one of despair and hopelessness. Her father had always been a rock, holding the family up no matter how difficult things got. He had stayed smiling and dry-eyed while her mother broke into tears as they said goodbye to Nick. Even Ashley started bawling, though she didn't seem to know why. Rachel started to tear up too, but her father stood there proud and strong. Now tears threatened to spill from his eyes, the mighty walls that held up the rest of the family starting to crack.

Because one member of the family was gone. Not simply away

at college, where a phone call or a plane ticket on the holidays could allow them to reconnect, but . . . gone.

"I need to find her," he said. "It's my job. That's what a dad does. He keeps the family together. He protects them, provides for them, supports them . . . I didn't do my job. I let Ashley get taken."

"Dad, there was nothing you could have done."

"I let her get taken!" he snapped, his arms shaking by his sides like wild dogs eager to hunt down and tear apart their prey, but which was nowhere to be found. "I failed to protect my baby girl and need to bring her home."

Her father jumped to his feet so fast that, for a brief and irrational moment, Rachel thought he was going to attack her. Of course, her father never lashed out at Rachel, and she felt stupid for thinking for a minute he would. Instead, he stomped off directionless, a loaded gun with no target to aim at. Rachel stood back, watching him wander down the path. Instead of heading to her mother in the car, he walked past, prowling the boundaries between the electric lights and the ever-present night. She knew he was scouting for the silhouette man, but she wasn't sure if it was for the better or for the worse that her dad didn't find him. No silhouette man meant they were safe, but it came at the cost of any hope of finding Ashley.

Not that Rachel thought they would. She didn't know what was happening, but a vague idea was forming. Before she could think about it, the payphone rang, calling her attention. She cocked her head and narrowed her eyes at the now-ringing phone. It rang and rang. She looked over her shoulder at her father, but he was too far away to hear it. That, or the ringing wasn't meant for him. It was just a hunch, but she didn't think her father would be able to hear it if he was standing right next to it. She walked up to the phone and reached for the handset but froze with her fingertips a hair's breadth from it. Taking a deep breath, she snatched the handset before her courage could abandon her.

"Hello?" she asked.

"Hey, sis," Nick's voice came through the tinny transmitter. "How are you doing? You having a day or what?"

The handset almost slipped from her hand, but Rachel recovered from the shock and clenched it so hard the plastic groaned in protest. "You aren't my brother."

"I'm not?" the voice from the phone said. "Then who am I?"

"You're him," Rachel said. "You're the silhouette man."

"The silhouette man," the thing using Nick's voice said. "Nice name. Sounds sinister. Silhouette man."

"Are you?" she asked. "Him?"

"No," the voice on the phone said. "Well, yes. Kind of. It's complicated."

"On top of everything else, you need to taunt me," Rachel growled into the phone.

"No, not at all," the thing pretending to be Nick said. "Believe me, that's not my intention."

"I don't care what your intention is. You took my sister!" she hissed, glancing over her shoulder to ensure her parents were out of earshot. "I want her back!"

"I'm afraid that's not possible," the fake Nick said, "but she's safe. She's waiting for you, in fact."

A lump formed in her chest, a budding hope. "I want to see her. Now."

"When you're ready," the thing on the phone said.

"I'm ready now!" Rachel shouted, forgetting herself. She glanced back to see her father staring at her with a puzzled look. He gave up looking for the silhouette man and started back up the path toward her.

"No, not quite yet," the voice of Nick said, "but you're getting there, I think."

Rachel gritted her teeth. This thing wanted to play games? Fine, she'd play. "Then what do I need to do to get ready?"

The voice on the other end of the phone stammered, "Eh, telling you would kind of defeat the purpose. You have to discover it on your own. Otherwise, you don't really discover it. You know what I mean? It's kind of a Zen thing."

"That's not funny." She forced her shouts down to a whisper as her father's footsteps drew closer.

"Think about it, Rachel," the voice said, "Think about the things that have been holding you back in life. The fears, the doubts, the regrets."

"What about them?"

"What attachments are weighing you down?"

Rachel's mind raced with a flurry of thoughts and emotions. She knew the voice on the other end was not really her brother's. It was something else, something more sinister.

"I want to see my sister," she said.

"Rachel?" her father called out to her. "Is the phone working? Can we call for help?"

"I know you do," the voice pretending to be Nick said. "Believe me, I feel for you. I do. It will all make sense eventually. You'll have to trust me on that."

"Trust you?" Rachel shouted, knowing that as her father drew nearer her time was growing short. "You took my sister! How am I supposed to trust you?"

"Rachel? Who are you talking to?" her father called out, his pace quickening.

"I didn't take anyone," the voice from the phone said. "I mean, technically, that wasn't me, but let's not play with semantics. The point is no one *took* your sister. She found her peace."

Rachel almost dropped the receiver. "You killed her?"

The voice on the phone laughed. "Oh, no. I think you know *I* didn't kill your sister."

"Rachel? Who is that?" Her father was beside her now, reaching for the phone, but Rachel twisted to keep it out of his reach.

"What happened to Ashley?" Rachel shouted.

"The same thing that happens to everyone," the voice said. "The same thing that will happen to your father, eventually. The same thing that will happen to you. What happened to your mother."

"What happens? What are you - ?" The change of tense hit her, stunning her long enough to enable her father to yank the phone from her hand. As her father called into the handset, however, Rachel pushed past him and ran back to the car.

There, by the car, under the glow of the streetlamp, stood her mother. Her arms were open as if waiting to be raptured into the air, but what she was waiting for didn't come from the sky.

The silhouette man stepped into the umbrella of light, forming a perfect cutout of pure black. He walked up to her mother, who just stood there waiting. Rachel screamed as she sprinted down the path. Her mother looked back over her shoulder at her, and while tears streaked down her face, she smiled. She heard her father running up behind her. It was happening all over again, just as it had with Ashley.

This time, though, Rachel reached her mother before the silhouette man did. She shoved her mother into the open car door as her father ran past, charging after the silhouette man. He swung at the man of darkness, but the silhouette man dissipated like smoke. Her father stumbled forward, his fist hitting nothing, the missing physical form throwing his gait off. Rachel spun around, looking for where the silhouette man had gone. She expected it to reform right behind her, but he was missing.

"Where did he go?" her father shouted with fists clenched.

"Never mind, let's just go!" Rachel screamed. She ran up to him and pulled him by the arm toward the car. "Let's get out of here before he comes back!"

"I want him to come back!" Then to the night, her father shouted, "Bring me back my daughter, you son-of-a-!"

Rachel jerked at her father's arm again, like it was the reigns of a horse trying to throw her. "Ashley is gone, Dad! If he comes back, Mom will be next!"

The thought of his wife in jeopardy slapped the righteousness out of him. He looked at her mother in the car, anger instantly replaced with fear and concern. Her mother, however, stared vacantly out the car window, past Rachel and her father, and out into the night. Her father's resistance melted, and Rachel shoved him to the driver's side door. He opened it and slid behind the wheel as if the seat was greased, pulling the seatbelt over himself in a fluid and well-practiced move, as Rachel jumped in the back seat. She didn't bother buckling up but leaned between the two front seats.

"Go!" she shouted. "Go, go, go!"

The front wheels of the SUV squealed as the car raced backward. Rachel clutched the seats hard to keep herself from being thrown through the front window. Then the car stopped hard, almost throwing Rachel back against the rear seat, testing Rachel's grip on the front seats, before rocketing forward again. The SUV threatened to roll over as it took the banking turn towards the freeway onramp, the headlights lighting up the road ahead of them.

Except where they hit the form of a featureless man standing in their way.

Her father slammed on the brakes, making him fight with the wheel to keep control of the car. It rocked back and forth on its shock absorbers until it came to a rest in front of the silhouette man. The beams from the headlights refused to touch him, like iron filings pushed away from a magnet. He stood there unmoving as if trying to block their path with his mere presence. The silhouette man cocked his head. It was impossible to tell with no facial features, but Rachel got the feeling it was looking right at her mother. Her mother's eyes fixed on the dark figure. Her expression was calm, peaceful, and accepting as if she had finally found the courage to face the inevitable. Her gaze was intense, almost hypnotic as if she were drawing the silhouette man towards her with an invisible force. Despite the chaos and fear around her, she radiated a sense of serenity and grace as if she had found a hidden source of strength within herself. Her eyes glowed with a warm, ethereal light, a sign of the transformation that had taken place within her. Rachel could sense her mother's resolve and courage, but also her own stubbornness and fear.

"Dad, back up," Rachel said.

"This is the only onramp to the freeway," her father growled.

"What about the way we came in?" Rachel asked.

"It's the wrong way," her father said. "We'd be driving into oncoming traffic-"

"There is no traffic!" Rachel screamed. "We're the only car on the road! Go!"

Her father sat there, clutching the steering wheel as he stared at the thing that took his daughter, deciding which instinct to surrender to – fight or flight. Then her father threw the car in reverse and stomped on the gas pedal. The SUV zoomed backward, the silhouette man swallowed up by the endless night. The SUV turned way too fast, the wheels on one side lifting from the ground as it fought against gravity and tried to roll onto its side. Gravity won, however, pulling all four wheels back onto the ground. Her father shifted the SUV into drive and sent the car racing in the wrong direction down the offramp. Rachel could tell her father was terrified that they would run head-first into an oncoming car, but that was the last thing she feared running into. There were no other cars on the road. Anywhere. Ever.

She leaned between the front seats and put her hand on her mother's shoulder. Her mother turned to Rachel with a look of serenity and a bittersweet smile and said, "I'll always love you."

"Mom?"

Before she could say any more, the headlights hit a spot in front of them that they couldn't penetrate. Ahead of them, standing in the center of the road waiting for them, was the silhouette man. Without taking the time to think, her father jerked the wheel hard to avoid hitting him, but the car was going too fast. Faster than she could scream out a warning, Rachel could tell the corner of the SUV would hit the silhouette man. Only the car never made contact. The silhouette man passed through the car like a ghost until it reached her mother. He wrapped his arms around her mother and went from immaterial to immutable in an eyeblink. The car ripped apart like tinfoil, the passenger door tearing off, her mother's seatbelt snapping like twine. The car spun, the silhouette man now an anchor, a black hole that the car orbited, and he was sucking in her mother.

The last thing Rachel saw as the car rolled over was the silhouette man hugging her mother to him and her mother sinking into him. She looked like she was curling up in a soft, warm bed, her eyes closed and her smile wide as she descended into the inky blackness of the silhouette man. Then the car was upside down and at an angle, rolling back up to flip again. Rachel was thrown around the car's interior, bouncing off Ashley's empty car seat as it was ripped from the car and flew out the hole in the side. The windows shattered, and chunks of thick glass rained down on her. She was thrown to the car's floor before being slammed against the roof, her father buried in the deployed airbag. Then she careened into the window of the door by her seat, her forehead smashing against the broken window, shards of glass impaling her flesh as she heard a sickening snap in her neck.

She bolted upright, strapped in her seat in the back. The car was back on the highway, swerving as her father snapped awake. Rachel and her father both looked around the intact car. All signs of the destruction that happened moments ago were gone.

Well, not all signs. Ashley's car seat sat empty, and now so did the front passenger seat.

"What the . . ?" her father sputtered. "Did . . . did we blackout? Grace?"

Rachel reached up to her head, where she hit the window. It still hurt. She could still feel the warm blood running down her forehead, blood that was now gone, the wound missing.

Her father twisted around in his seat. "Grace? Rachel, where's your mother?"

"She's gone, Dad," Rachel said.

A heavy blanket of silence draped over them, broken only by the engine's hum. Then the tires squealed as her father turned hard to the left, taking the SUV off the road and into the center median. The top-heavy SUV bounced in the dirt, losing speed and leaning dangerously to the side.

"Dad, what -?"

"Going back to get your mother and your sister," her father said as the SUV pulled onto the asphalt of the opposite lane.

Rachel unbuckled her seatbelt and climbed between the front seats, sliding into her mother's spot beside her father. Peering out the windshield, the way they came looked as empty as the way they had been going, except for the single light gleaming from behind the steel billboard column on the side of the road now opposite them. As they started to pass it, Rachel saw the source of the single light for the first time.

It came from a single car headlight, the other buried between the steel column and the crumpled front end of a large car.

"Dad, stop the car," Rachel said.

"What?"

"There's a car accident." She pointed across her father to the car they were passing.

As they passed, her father looked at the wreck, biting his lower lip. Rachel knew he wanted to stop and help, thinking of what it would be like if he was in the crashed car with his family waiting for help, but then he shook his head. "No, we have our own problems right now."

"Dad, you don't get it -"

"I get that your mother and sister have been kidnapped," her father said, cutting her off.

Her father didn't get it, but Rachel thought she was beginning to. She gripped the handle to the door and froze. Was she sure about this? If she was right, they had to get to the car. If she was wrong . . . well, she might not live to regret her decision. Every second of indecision, though, meant they were moving farther away from the wrecked car. Taking a deep breath, Rachel pulled the handle to the car door and jumped. The wind whipped her hair around her face, and the world became a blur. The impact with the ground was sudden and jarring, forcing all the air from her lungs. She tumbled head over heels, her body bouncing and rolling along the pavement. She lay there in the dark for a moment, her lungs struggling to suck in air again. In the distance, she heard the squealing tires of the SUV as her father hit the brakes, the vehicle's taillights shining brightly in the night.

Slowly, her aching lungs found their rhythm, taking in cold dust-filled air. The SUV had been going . . . what? Sixty? Not with her father in the panic that was gripping him. She guessed at least eighty. Colliding with the ground hurt, but it should have broken every bone in her body. She should be a bloody pulp on the ground, but she was fine. Aching all over, but in one piece. She thought she knew why.

In the distance, her father jumped out of the SUV. "Rachel!"

Her father froze when she stood up, confusion overriding his parental concern for his daughter's safety. Before her father could recover, Rachel pivoted to the car crash and started across the highway.

"Rachel!" Her father raced after her while turning his head from side to side, looking for oncoming traffic. Rachel didn't bother. She knew there would be no speeding cars on the freeway to dodge. They were well past the accident scene when Rachel jumped, so she ran to the twin taillights glowing back at her like the eyes of a demon. When she got close enough to make out the vehicle in the darkness, she came to a halt. She stood there, staring at the back of another SUV, when her father came up and grabbed her arm.

"What the hell do you think you're doing?" her father shouted. "Do you know have any idea how dangerous that was?"

"Dad," Rachel said, not taking her eyes off the back of the crashed SUV. She could smell the metallic-tinged steam escaping from the cracked radiator. "Look."

"You could have gotten yourself killed!" her father said, continuing his chastising. "If there had been a car, they would never have seen you -"

"Dad!" Rachel shouted, pointing at the SUV. "Look!"

This time, her father did look at the back of the SUV, the same make and model as their own. No, it was more than that. Rachel couldn't have told her father what their license plate number was from memory, but she had no doubt that she was looking at it now, illuminated by the glow of a single light built into the frame. She didn't want to go any closer to the SUV – *their* SUV – but she needed answers. No, that wasn't true, not if she was being honest with herself. She knew the truth. Looking into the car would be confirming it, would be accepting it. Her heart was racing like a hummingbird's, but she forced herself to take a step toward the car. Her father reached out for her, but his grip had no strength. He stayed where he was as if some invisible force field was pushing him back.

Rachel walked up to the rear driver's side window. It was

spiderwebbed, red blood filling the cracks in the glass. Smooshed up against the broken window, matted with blood, was a mass of brown hair. Brown, that was, except for the streak of pink that was now stained with dried blood.

"Rachel?" her father called out. "Come back. We can go get help. We can find a phone -"

"It's us, Dad." She tried to call out for her father to hear her, but she could barely breathe.

"What? What do you mean?"

Rachel pulled out her phone and turned on the flashlight app. The light shone into her doppelganger's eyes, which were open but seeing nothing. Her father's face – the one in the car – rested on the deflated airbag, but the SUV must have been going faster than the airbag could counteract. Her mother, however, didn't stand a ghost of a chance. It was her corner of the car that impacted the steel column of the billboard. That part of the car was just gone, ripped apart like the vehicle was made of tin foil. The passenger-side airbag did its best to protect her mother, but it was outmatched by the force of the impact. Her mother's face took the brunt, smashed beyond anything resembling a human being. Blood and small chunks of flesh were splattered across the dashboard and windshield. She swallowed hard and aimed the light at Ashley. She didn't think she could bear seeing the baby's bloodied and mangled body, but Ashley was unmarked. Her body was slumped in the car seat. She could have been sleeping if it wasn't for the unhealthy shade of blue tinging her skin. Rachel guessed the impact had snapped the baby's neck, killing her instantly.

Rachel's lips began to quiver, her eyes blurring as the tears built up, but she couldn't look away. She wanted to. She didn't want to see them – see herself – like this, but to look away would be . . . what? Disrespectful, somehow? Like denying their deaths? Her death?

"Rachel?" her father called out to her. He still stood back from the car, waving for her to join him. "Come away from that. You don't need to see things like that."

"Did you know?" she asked.

"What are you talking about?"

She pointed to the car. "It's us, Dad! That's us in the car! We're dead!"

Her father scrunched up his face in confusion. He walked up and took her arm, not looking into the car. "What? No, we can't be. We're right here. Rachel, step away from them."

She threw his hand off her. "What are you doing?"

"You don't need to be seeing things like this," he said. "It's my job to protect you from things like seeing that. I'm your father."

"We're dead, Dad," she said. "You can't protect me from being dead."

"We aren't dead. We're right here arguing!" her father shouted. "And I'm your father. I'll protect you from everything, so don't give me that!"

Rachel threw up her hands. "What are we going to do, Dad? Keep driving down this highway over and over for all eternity?"

"Eternity," her father scoffed. "We're almost home."

"We're never getting home!" Rachel screamed. Hysteria

threatened to overtake her, but once she said it, a strange sense of calm washed over her. "We're never getting home."

"Rachel."

"We don't have a choice," she said. "We have to move on. It's not up to us. Not anymore."

"No, we're not moving on," her father said. "We aren't dead. We're talking. We're breathing. We are alive."

She smiled at her father, the same bittersweet smile her mother gave her before vanishing. Then she turned. She wasn't surprised to see the silhouette man cutting into the cone of light from the lone headlight. She stepped toward him. "We need to pass on, don't we?"

The silhouette man said nothing but gave a single nod.

"Don't!" her father called out, but he was rooted to the spot. "Stay. I'll look after you. I'll protect you. I'm your dad."

Tears rolled down her face as she looked back over her shoulder toward her father. "I get it now. Change happens. It's just a part of life." Then she turned back to the silhouette man. "And mine's over, isn't it?"

The silhouette man said nothing. As Rachel stepped closer, he opened his arms wide, welcoming her. The last thing Rachel heard before vanishing into the silhouette man was her father calling out to her.

She thought that would be it, that she would fade into oblivion, but the darkness faded into never-ending bright blue skies. It was like she was standing on glass, casting a blurred reflection of this new world. Standing before her was her mother, holding Ashley in her arms. Rachel couldn't remember ever being happier to see either of them. She ran to them, wrapping her arms around them and crying against her mother's chest.

"I thought you were gone," Rachel sobbed. "I thought I'd never see either of you again."

Her mother caressed her head. "It's like I tried to tell you, Princess. We may move away, but we will never leave you. Not in a way it matters."

Rachel looked back at the way she came. The silhouette man stood there, but now, instead of being an inky black, he was a bright and glowing white. "What about Dad?"

"Your dad might need some more time before he's ready," her mother said, unable to hide the heaviness in her voice.

"What do we do?" Rachel asked.

Her mother wrapped her free arm around Rachel's shoulder, Ashley babbling happily in the other. "We wait. We stand by him, whether he knows we're here for him or not, and hope he finds his way to us."

Jim awoke behind the wheel of the family SUV. The fear of realizing he had nodded off while the car ran down the highway sent a jolt like electricity through his heart. The car was drifting and going recklessly fast. He yanked the wheel and almost overcompensated. He fought the weaving car and regained control.

"Sorry," he called out. "Everything's okay."

Except he was talking to an empty car. He looked over, both

expecting to see Grace sitting next to him, and knowing she was gone. He reached up and angled the rearview mirror to see the empty seats in the back. Something had taken his family, and he had to get them back. He hit the info screen on his car, the system linked to his phone, and tried to dial the police. He tried dialing his son, Nick, who was undoubtedly asleep in his dorm room by now. He tried to dial anyone, but the phone refused to connect with the network. He didn't even get that recorded message that his call "couldn't be completed as dialed." There was just . . . nothing.

Jim punched the info screen and screamed. The info screen fractured, tinted with blood from his cut knuckles. He needed to find a working phone. He needed to get help, to find his family, to get the man who took them. It was his family. That was his responsibility, his duty, to make sure nothing happened to them. He failed, both as a father and as a husband, but he would find them. He would save them. He would drive all night if he needed to, but he wouldn't have to. He just needed to find a working phone. Then he'd call the police, the FBI, the National Guard, and whoever else he needed to find his family. All he needed was to find a phone.

Up ahead, Jim saw the bright lights of a rest stop cutting through the darkness. He'd pull over and find a good old-fashioned pay phone. If that didn't work, he'd keep driving until he found a gas station or a roadside diner. If that failed . . . well, he'd just keep driving. He only had a few hours left to go anyway.

He was almost home.

FAMILY

It was a bright spring day. The grass was green and lush, and the cool mountain air, chilled even more by the ocean, kept the temperature comfortable. It would have been the perfect day for a picnic. Unfortunately, while being on a picturesque cliff overlooking the Pacific, the graveyard was a poor location for one, and the funeral dampened the mood.

Anna watched the funeral from a distance, standing under a tall pine tree. Beside her, holding her hand, Bethany shifted her weight repeatedly. Anna squeezed her daughter's hand, silently telling her she understood Bethany's boredom and fatigue. It also reassured Anna herself, like a pocket-sized hug. With her free hand, Anna wiped the tears from her eyes. The wind carried the eulogy to her, and she could just make it out over the rustling of the grass and the pine needles.

"Mommy?" Bethany said, looking up at her mother. "I'm sorry you're so sad."

She let go of Bethany's hand so she could hug her daughter close. Anna ran her hand down Bethany's straight brown hair, so much like her father's. She sniffled, then said, "It's okay, baby."

"Why are we all the way over here?" Bethany asked. "Everyone is over there."

"You know why," Anna said. "We talked about this."

Bethany lapsed back into silence. Anna knew it was hard for Bethany to understand. After six years, Anna still didn't understand herself. After all this time, however, the hiding and false identities were a way of life, so much so that coming to the funeral was making her very anxious. This was the opposite of what over half a decade of honed instinct told her she should be doing.

Even if the funeral was for her father.

Especially because it was for her father.

Lost in her thoughts, Anna didn't notice the funeral was ending until the eulogy came to a close and the coffin was being lowered into the fresh grave. The mourners started to disperse slowly, as those grieving were prone to do. Anna cursed herself. She meant to leave sooner to avoid people who would recognize her. She could spot several familiar faces in the crowd. Before she could turn and run, she saw Mark standing by the lowering coffin. Her heart ached for him, not just because he was saying goodbye to their father, but because he was doing it alone. She should be there beside her brother, the two siblings sharing their sorrow together instead of hiding by a tree twenty yards away.

Then Mark turned. Even at this distance, Anna could read the shock and puzzlement on his face as he looked right at her. Anna cursed out loud, earning her a wide-eyed look of shock from Bethany. She pulled her by the hand and darted behind the tree. "We need to go. Now."

"But Mommy," Bethany said, leaning back and using all her weight like an anchor. "You said you wanted to say goodbye to your daddy. I didn't even meet your daddy yet."

Anna knelt and picked Bethany up into her arms. Bethany wasn't an infant anymore, but at five she wasn't too big for Anna to carry, at least for a little while. "I told you, baby, we can't be seen."

She started to leave, but other departing mourners started walking past, forcing her to duck back behind the tree to keep from being noticed. She didn't recognize the people walking by, but she couldn't take the chance they might recognize her. She had been hiding from everyone for six years, though that didn't keep her brother from picking her out in a crowd, and some of the older folks had long memories. As more of the funeral attendees made their way out of the graveyard, Anna slunk around the other side of the tree, looking for an escape route.

And walked right into Mark, leaning against the tree, and waiting for her.

Bethany busied herself with the kids' menu, coloring in the

picture with the crayons pulled out of a tin can covered with decades of stray marks. The adults sat opposite each other, neither of them talking. Anna kept glancing around, wondering who else would spot her. She felt vulnerable, like a turtle out of its shell. She looked at Mark and his relentless glare.

"What?" she asked.

"Just waiting for you to explain," Mark said. "You have a kid! How did you get a kid? I mean, I know *how* -"

"Mark."

Bethany looked up from her coloring, her eyes wide and her face blank, the universal expression of a child who hadn't done anything wrong but wondered if she was in trouble anyway. "How do you get a kid?"

Anna shot Mark a warning glare, but he ignored it. "Six years. We've been looking for you for six years."

Anna's heart sank into her stomach. "Us?"

"Me. Dad," Mark said, then added, "Daniel."

Bethany didn't glance up at Daniel's name, but her lack of reaction earned one from Mark. Anna shot him another warning stare. "Don't."

"Don't you think he should know?" Mark asked, pointing at Bethany with a quick dart of his eyes. Anna swallowed hard as she shot her own glance at her daughter, but Bethany was blissfully ignorant of the adult's conversation, too engrossed in her art project.

"He can't know," Anna said.

"Why not?" Mark asked. The eyes of both adults drifted back

to Bethany, then back to each other. Mark held up a finger, then fished his phone out of his pocket along with a set of headphones. He fiddled with the phone for a moment, then handed it to Bethany. "Hey, you want to watch some cartoons?"

Bethany's eyes lit up and she nodded her head. Taking her cue from Mark, Anna took the headphones from him and placed them on Bethany's ears. "You have to keep the headphones on, though, okay? Because we're in a public place and we have to be respectful of other people, okay?"

"Okay, Mommy," she said, her attention already glued to the screen.

With Bethany settled, Mark said, "So, talk. What's this about?"

Anna checked to make sure Bethany was focused on her cartoon, then leaned across the table and whispered to Mark, "The day I found out I was pregnant, I was on my way to tell Daniel, but then this old woman stopped me in the parking lot and told me not to."

"Seriously?" Mark asked. "That has got to be the stupidest story I ever heard."

"Mark, you don't understand."

"Some random old woman gives you some weird advice, and you throw your life away?" Mark asked. "Do you have any idea what Daniel's been -?"

"She wasn't some random old woman. She claimed to be like my great-grandmother or something like that. She told me -" She looked at Bethany to make sure she was still safely ignorant of the adult conversation. Bethany was smiling, her eyes glued on the screen. Anna leaned toward Mark. "She told me I had to keep Bethany away from Daniel."

"Why?" Mark said.

"I don't know," Anna said, "but it's something bad."

"Oh, good, for the minute I thought you upended your life and alienated your family for something silly," Mark said dryly. "For crying out loud, Anna. This isn't like you. Well, not like the Anna I used to know. I don't recognize you anymore. I'm supposed to look out for you, but that's hard to do when you disappear on us."

Anna cocked an eyebrow. "I'm the older one. I'm supposed to look after you."

"Don't you remember what Dad always said?" Mark then dropped his voice in a mock parental tone. "Always look after your sister!"

"I'm not a damsel in distress," Anna said. "I can take care of myself."

"Well, I think Dad was a bit old-fashioned."

"That's a polite way of saying misogynistic."

"Maybe," Mark said, "but he cared about you. He wanted you safe more than anything else. He drilled that into my head — look after your sister, protect your sister, that's why God gave her a brother. Only now, you take your cues from some mysterious old woman? Seriously?"

Anna looked across the table at her brother, her hands nervously fiddling with the edge of her napkin. "She visited me a few different times over the years. She was there when Bethany was born.

I think she knew I was thinking of calling Daniel. I wanted him to be there with us so badly, but before I could work up the courage to call him, I fell asleep."

"Glad your troubled soul didn't give you insomnia," Mark said.

"Shut up. You try undergoing sixteen hours of labor," Anna snapped. "Point is, when I woke up to feed Bethany, she was there. The old woman. She was standing there in a corner like a living shadow. It was like she knew what I was thinking. She told me Bethany was the key."

Mark shrugged his shoulders. "The key to what?"

"It means she's the latest in a line of women bearing a curse," Anna said. "According to the old woman, everyone in our lineage gives birth to one and only one daughter. That daughter is the next key. Mark, you have to believe me. Bethany is the key, the one I've been cursed to give birth to."

Mark leaned back in his booth seat, arms folded across his chest. "Anna, I want to believe you, but it doesn't make sense."

"I know it's hard to believe -"

"No, I mean it logically doesn't make sense. I mean, hello?" Mark pointed to himself. "If any of that was true, how could Mom have given birth to me?"

Anna's eyes flickered with uncertainty. Mark was right. Why hadn't that occurred to her before? "I don't know. Maybe the curse skips a generation or something."

Mark shook his head. "That doesn't make any sense. You were convinced that Bethany was the key. That's why you've been hiding her from everyone, including her father. But if that were true, Mom wouldn't have been able to give birth to me, and you would have been an only child."

Anna's heart sank. Mark was right. Her entire belief system for the past six years had been built on the assumption that Bethany was the key, but if that were true, then there was a gaping hole in the curse's history.

"Maybe the old woman was wrong," Anna said weakly.

"Maybe the old woman is a liar and a crazy person. I don't know who she is, but I'm your family, not her." Mark let out a heavy sigh and sunk down in his booth. "And right now, you're the only family I have left."

Anna nodded, feeling a sense of resignation settle over her. She had thought she had everything figured out and was doing what was best for her daughter. But now she realized that she didn't know anything at all. The key, the curse, the old woman - it was all a jumbled mess in her mind.

As they sat in silence, except for the muted sound of Bethany's cartoons humming from the headphones, Anna couldn't help but feel a sense of dread wash over her. What if she had been wrong about everything? What if there was no curse, no key, no old woman? What if it was all just in her head? She didn't know if she could handle the truth if it turned out that way.

A thought hit her. "What happened to the house?"

"What house?"

"The White House," Anna said. "What house do you think I

mean? Our house. Dad's house."

Mark shrugged. "Nothing. It's just sitting there empty."

Her heart sank. The thought of the house she had grown up in stripped to the baseboards, sitting bare and waiting for new owners depressed her almost as much as losing her father. Worse, though, was the treasure trove of personal history piled up in a dump where only the flies could find them. Maybe everything was taken to a thrift store or, even better, a storage unit? "Where did everything go?"

"What everything?" Mark asked.

Anna clenched her eyes and jaw shut as she forced herself to remain calm. She had forgotten how annoyingly obtuse Mark could be. "Everything from our house. The photo albums, passports, birth certificates -"

"Oh, that?" Mark asked, the proverbial light bulb coming on over his head. "Nah, all that stuff is still there. I have been so busy with the funeral I haven't had a chance to deal with Dad's estate." He said the last words in a stuffy, hoity-toity voice, as if "estate" was a fancy word. Then he cocked an eyebrow at Anna. "I was dealing with Dad's death by myself, after all."

"You said it was empty."

Mark nodded. "I meant of people. No one is living there. It's just all the stuff."

Anna looked at Bethany, giggling at cartoons on Mark's phone. Then she looked back up to Mark. "Can you watch Bethany for a bit?"

"Now you trust me with your kid?" Mark asked with a hint of a smirk.

"It wasn't like that," Anna said, "and I don't have a choice. Take her back to your place and keep out of sight."

"Who do you think is going to recognize her?" Mark asked.

"Just . . . can you?" Anna asked.

Mark shrugged, then smiled. "Sure. Gives me time to get to know my niece, who I never knew existed until today."

Anna growled at Mark, but he flashed her a smug grin. He knew she needed him, so he had the advantage. Instead of going down the rabbit hole of sibling bickering, she turned to Bethany. Anna tapped her on her shoulder, and Bethany pulled the headphones off and looked up at Anna.

"These cartoons are really funny, Mommy," she said.

"Baby," Anna said. "I need you to go with your Uncle Mark for a little bit, okay?"

Bethany looked at her mother with a mixture of puzzlement and concern, her eyes wide and her mouth pursed, like her mother said she was going to abandon her. To say Bethany was on the verge of tears was an exaggeration, but she was verge adjacent.

"It'll be fun, kid," Mark said, calling Bethany's attention. He flashed her a crooked smile and a wink. "I'll tell you all the embarrassing stories of your mother from when she was a kid."

The wider Bethnay's devilish smile grew, the more Anna regretted this idea.

Anna parked her car some distance from her father's house, pulling off the road and tucking it between the trees. She hiked her way through the woods instead of taking the road. She asked herself, were all these precautions needed anymore? Were they ever needed, or had the old woman made a mistake all those years ago? She wasn't sure if she should feel angry or relieved at that idea. All the years of hiding, having left Daniel and everyone she knew, and to think it might have been for nothing? Then again, what if it was over? What if she and Bethany were safe, if there was no unnamed threat looming over them after all?

The paths she had known as a child were still there. Though recognizable, they weren't exactly as she remembered them. She wondered how much of that was because the forest had changed or because she had. The overgrown brush reached out and scratched red angry marks all over her arms. The path led her right where she expected, to the back of the house. On the other side of the house, the tall trees muffled the sound of the occasional car or lumbar-hauling diesel truck except for the hole in the tree line where a long gravel driveway connected it to the main road. It was a double-edged sword. The seclusion would keep anyone from spotting her, but it also kept her from being able to spot anyone approaching.

Her key still worked on the back door. Anna slipped it back into her pocket, and as she stepped inside she was hit with stale air and nostalgia. Dust danced in the beams of sunlight that snuck between the branches of the tall trees outside. The house was almost unchanged from the last time she had been here. Hung on the walls were pictures of her family – she and Mark dressed for Halloween, her father and pregnant mother holding a baby Anna, and the portrait of her mother that her father hung after her death. Looking at the old photos for the first time in years, she saw a deep-rooted undertone of sadness in her father's expressions. Anna couldn't say she had never noticed it before, but it was like how she was unaware of her own breathing until she was asked to inhale deeply under the cold metal of a doctor's stethoscope. Now, though, it was stark and obvious. There was a different but just as ever-present look on her mother's face too. Her smile was bitter-sweet like the idealistic life the photos captured came at a cost. It was happiness tinged with . . . what? Guilt? Sadness? It was hard to tell.

Anna traced her fingers along the familiar books on the shelves. She wasn't sure what she was looking for, but she didn't think she'd find it in the parts of the house familiar to her. If there were some profound, dark family secret, it wouldn't be sitting on the bookshelf in the living room. She looked up at the stairwell toward her father's bedroom. The polished wooden steps creaked as she made her way upstairs. Reaching the second-floor landing, she felt the pull of her old room, but she knew there would be no answers for her there. She also recognized her desire to visit her childhood bedroom as what it was. A distraction. Something to put off entering her father's room.

She couldn't remember when it stopped being her parents' room and became her father's room. Even after her mother's death, it was still her parents' room for years. Then, like the coming of night, her mother's presence faded until one day, it was just gone. She stood in the doorway, looking at the made bed and one nightstand covered with prescription pill bottles. The mattress was lopsided, the side by the cluttered nightstand lower than the other. Anna took in a shuddering breath as she realized it was because, until the day he died, her father still slept on his side of the bed, as if someday her mother would return to them. Return to him.

Anna searched the room. Slowly, at first, with a sense of reverence, but every drawer she sifted through encouraged her to search the next one a bit more quickly and a bit more aggressively. After going through his dresser, Anna got to know her father's choice of underwear better than she cared too. The only thing odd she found on his nightstand was a key with a strange and intricate emblem in the head, an ornate triangle in a circle with what looked like writing all around the edges, but in a language she didn't recognize. However, nothing in her father's bedroom had a lock on it, so she had no idea what it might open. She found her mother's wedding dress in the closet in a protective plastic bag. All her mother's other clothes were long gone, but her father kept her wedding dress all this time. Did he keep it for Anna? Staring at it, Anna couldn't remember a single photo of her mother wearing it. For that matter, the dress looked to be too long for her mother, but it was hard to say for sure.

In the end, she found nothing of importance in her father's bedroom. No hidden safe full of fake passports was found behind a painting or cache of birth certificates under the mattress. Frustrated, she left her father's room and stood in the hall. Glancing around, wondering what to do next, she saw the cord for the folded attic stairs hanging from the ceiling. It was out of her reach, so she had to run back downstairs, grab a dining room chair, and haul it up to the second floor. By the time she pulled the folding ladder down and climbed into the musty attic, she was breathing heavily. She pulled out her phone and turned on the flashlight app, taking in her surroundings while catching her breath.

Everything was a brownish-grey, from the stacks of cardboard boxes to the bare wood planks serving as the attic's floor. None of the boxes were marked, so she began opening up the boxes at random. She spent over an hour sorting through holiday decorations and old tax records. She must have gone through every cardboard box in the attic before she found it. It was a chest with years of dust collected on it. Trying to pull it open, Anna found it was locked. Brushing the caked filth off the front lock, she could make out a familiar triangle-over-a-circle symbol engraved on the lock. She raced back down the stairs to her father's bedroom, pulled open the nightstand drawer, and grabbed the key with the matching emblem. She darted back up the creaking attic stairs to the chest and slipped the key in. Despite its age and neglect, the lock opened without effort.

Anna fished through the contents. Underneath some papers was a framed photograph. A woman sat in a luxurious Queen Anne chair holding a baby. Standing behind her with an arm around her shoulder was her father. He was younger than Anna had ever seen, even in photos, but it was unmistakably her father. The odd part was that her mother was also in the picture. She stood with her hands clasped together, standing stiffly behind the woman in the chair opposite her father. She flipped the picture over, pulled off the backing, and examined the photo. Written in the corner were "Charles,

Charlotte, and Anna," followed by a date a few weeks after her birthday.

"Charlotte?" Anna asked. Her mother didn't even warrant having her name written down. She flipped it back over and stared at the woman in the chair, the woman holding her. "Who are you?"

She put the photo down and rummaged through the trunk some more. Buried deep in the chest under more photos and papers was a book, the cover worn leather, the pages yellowed with age. Anna made herself as comfortable as possible on the rough attic floor and began reading.

Charlotte held Anna against her chest and just watched her sleep. Was there ever a baby as beautiful as her Anna? She figured every mother in history thought that, but in her case, it had to be true. She caressed the baby's nearly bald head and smiled as she sat in the large-backed Queen Anne chair. She nuzzled her daughter and took in her scent, but the new-baby aroma mixed with the perfume of the photographer. The fragrance wasn't unpleasant, a fresh spring scent, but it was intrusive and unwelcome.

"Charlotte, dear?" her husband, Charles, said, calling her attention away from Anna. She looked up at Charles's stern yet not unkind face looking down at the two of them. He was a handsome man but always so serious. She couldn't fault him for that, though. He carried a lot on his shoulders. More, now that Anna was born.

Her husband directed his glance to the photographer standing in front of them. Charlotte sat upright, readying her pose, but she heard the rustling of clothes behind her and on the opposite side of the chair from Charles. She looked over her shoulder to see Rebecca stepping out of frame. She reached out and took Rebecca's hand, careful not to jostle the sleeping Anna in her other arm.

"Rebecca, stay," Charlotte said.

Rebecca froze, glancing down at Charlotte but not quite meeting her eyes. Her glance flitted to Charles before darting back to Charlotte.

"Really, dear," Charles said. He didn't shout, but his deep voice resonated in the small room. "This is a family portrait."

Charlotte gave Rebecca's hand a squeeze. "Rebecca is part of our family. Please, Rebecca, stay."

Again, her eyes shifted between her and Charles, snapping back to Charlotte in a blink. "Yes, of course."

Rebecca stepped back and took her position behind and to the left of Charlotte, who sat up straight for the camerawoman. The photographer took the picture several times, then stepped out from behind the camera. She had silky black hair braided in a ponytail that draped past her shoulders, and flawless light-brown skin. Her dark brown eyes locked on Anna for a heartbeat too long, and Charlotte squeezed Anna tighter to herself. The photographer flashed Charlotte a warm smile.

"She's such a beautiful baby," she said.

Charlotte returned the smile, though she didn't feel at all cheerful. "Thank you."

"Well, I should have what I need," she said. "I'll get this

developed and to you folks in a few days."

Charlotte looked back down at the sleeping baby in her arms. In a soft voice, she said, "Come on, little Anna. Time to get you to bed."

As Charlotte shuffled to get to her feet while her arms were full holding her baby, Rebecca bent over and reached for Anna. "Let me take her."

"It's fine, Rebecca, I -"

"Let Rebecca do her job, Charlotte," Charlie said. "It is what we hired her for."

Charlotte clenched her teeth. Her husband was right, of course, but he didn't need to be so blunt about it. She hadn't chosen to hire Rebecca at random. Until she met Charles, Rebecca was the closest thing she had to a friend. Before meeting Rebecca, she had kept to herself, leading a solitary life.

It's what the old woman told her to do.

But humans are social creatures, and she struggled with isolation. She kept Rebecca as distant as she could, but the need for human companionship was too great to deny. The only force even stronger, she would learn, after meeting Charles, was love. They married and soon were expecting. In choosing a nanny for little Anna, there was only one person Charlotte could trust.

Charlotte handed Anna to Rebecca and immediately felt her daughter's absence. It was like the temperature in the room dropped ten degrees as her heart clenched into a fist. Still, Charles was right. She was still healing from the labor, still weak from bleeding that had not yet stopped. It was nothing to worry about, or so the physician reassured her on his daily visit to the house. While it was heavier than expected, there were no signs that the bleeding was anything to be too concerned about. It left her so weak, though, which led to the need for a nanny for Anna and their hiring Rebecca.

"Don't worry," Rebecca said, cradling the sleeping Anna. "I'll care for her as if she were my own."

Charlotte smiled up at her. "Of course, you will. I trust you completely."

"Are you okay," Charles asked her.

Charlotte forced a smile and nodded. "Yes. Just tired."

"Do you need anything?"

Charlotte shook her head, an act she immediately regretted. It made her a tad lightheaded. "I just need to sit for a bit. I'll be fine."

"Okay," Charles said. "I'll go with Rebecca to tuck our daughter in, then I'll be right back."

She reached up and squeezed Charles's hand. "Take your time. She won't be this little for very long. Enjoy it while you can."

Charles squeezed her hand back, then let go to follow Rebecca out of the room as the photographer packed up her gear. She turned off the large lights that had bathed the room in a diffused, uniform light. Now the late-day sun cast the room in a contrast of highlights and shadows. Once the lights were broken down and put in the case with the rest of her gear, the photographer hoisted it on her shoulder and said her goodbyes. Charlotte was glad to see her leave. She couldn't say why. The photographer had been nothing but cordial and professional, but something about how she kept shifting her glance at her and Anna made her uneasy. Charlotte chided herself for being so irrational. Were all new mothers so paranoid? At least she had Rebecca to lean on and to keep her level-headed.

Charlotte, now alone, leaned back in the plush chair and closed her eyes. She could hear the birds singing and splashing about in the large marble bird bath that sat outside in the large circular driveway leading up to the house. The lingering traces of the photographer's perfume hung in the air, a scent that reminded her of roses and springtime. She almost drifted off into sleep when she heard a familiar voice.

"You have no idea what you have done. Foolish girl."

Charlotte didn't open her eyes, as if the old woman was a bad dream and she could will her away. She had no idea what her name was, but the old woman had visited her many times over the years, usually with cryptic warnings. Charlotte didn't think today would be any different. "I know what I did. I got married and started a family."

"You lost any protection you had," the old woman said. "Yesterday's key is today's forge."

"I don't care about your riddles anymore," Charlotte said. "Charles and I are married, and we have a beautiful baby girl. Soon this house will be filled with children - "

"No, it won't."

The old woman's words felt like a needle piercing Charlotte's heart, and her eyes popped open. "Who are you to say - ?"

"It is the curse of our lineage," the old woman said. "You were the key, the one person to complete the last rite, but you got pregnant. At that point, you went from being the key to becoming the forge. Now your daughter is the key, and she will be the only key until your daughter continues the cycle, or she is used to complete the last rite. The forge has served its purpose, its furnace has cooled. You will have no other children."

Charlotte shot to her feet and spun to face the old woman. She found the wrinkled old woman standing in the shadows, hunched over as if she couldn't bear her own weight. Glaring at her, Charlotte spat, "If she's the only child I'll have, then I'll love her more than any child has ever been loved."

"You fail to comprehend the gravity of your situation," the old woman growled. "I did my best to hide you, but they can smell the new key fresh from the forge. They will be on you soon enough."

"Who?"

"Those who want to use the last rite to open the doorway and allow the dark ones in," the old woman said. "The ones who want to burn the world to ashes."

Charlotte scoffed. "Name one person who would want that?"

The old woman wiped the incredulous look off Charlotte's face with the raising of a single eyebrow. "I never said they were people."

Charlotte tried to laugh off such a ridiculous idea, but the unwavering glare from the old woman robbed her of any conviction. She had been doing that all Charlotte's life, telling the most outrageous tales in a way that left no room to doubt her. Charlotte found her hand clutching her chest as if someone else had placed it there. She dropped her hand, her arms folded across her chest in an attempt to project some semblance of authority. "No one is harming my daughter."

"This is not a fight you can win," the old woman said, "but I know some people who might be of some help in hiding you."

"Charles isn't the kind of man to hide," Charlotte said.

"Then he'll die," the old woman said. "The choice is his. It will be up to you to convince him."

"You could talk to him," Charlotte started to say, but the old woman silenced her with a gesture.

"Your husband is not my concern," she said. "Only that the last rite is not performed by those that would bring about the end."

"The end?" Charlotte asked. "The end of what?"

"Everything."

Charlotte swallowed her fear. "But these friends of yours can help?"

"I didn't say they were friends," the old woman said. "Their goals align with mine . . . usually. I find them useful allies, but they aren't without their own agendas."

"Can I trust them?" Charlotte asked.

"We don't have a choice," the old woman said, "but there is one amongst them I trust more than the others. An adjunct professor named Shayan Lightfoot."

"When will he be here?" Charlotte asked.

The old woman looked over her shoulder and stared into the shadows. "Not soon enough."

Charlotte opened her mouth to say something, but her words evaporated from her tongue. She heard something coming from the shadows, something like whispers. She could only make out indistinct mumblings at first, but listening hard, she could make out what sounded like words in a language she couldn't recognize. She backed away from the shadows, never taking her eyes off the dark corners of the room, but not seeing anything. The old woman stood there, not unnerved by the disembodied whispers. As she stepped out of the room, Charlotte thought she saw the shadows shift, like they were alive.

She ran through the house and up the ornate stairwell to where the bedrooms were. The further she got from the old woman, the more she calmed down, and her thinking grew more rational. It was like the old woman cast a spell on her, one that waned the further Charlotte got from her. By the time she reached the top of the stairs, she was embarrassed to have bought into the old woman's story. At the bottom of the stairs, she had been running to warn Charles of the nebulous threat the old woman had warned her about. Now she was looking for Charles to help stand up to her. She walked up along the hall to the nursery, but as she got closer, she heard Charles and Rebecca.

"If you aren't happy with me being here, I can leave," Rebecca said.

"Charlotte likes you being here," Charlies said, "and you're great with Anna."

"But what about you?" Rebecca asked. "Are you happy with me? Being here, I mean."

Charlotte stopped outside the nursery and pressed her back against the wall, breathing as shallowly as possible to not be heard as Charles said, "Why wouldn't I be happy with you here?"

"It's just . . . I mean . . . with our past and all," Rebecca said.

Charlotte held a hand to her mouth. Rebecca had introduced her to Charles, but she had no idea they were anything but acquaintances. What relationship did they used to have?

"That was before meeting Charlotte," Charles said.

"So, you're saying you no longer have feelings for me?" Rebecca asked.

"It's not that . . . I mean . . . I still care for you," Charles stammered. "But I love Charlotte."

"You used to say you loved me." Charlotte could hear the tears Rebecca was choking back.

"I did," he said. "I do. But I love Charlotte more, and I think you do too."

"Why else would I come here?" she asked. "You think it's easy to watch you and Charlotte together, knowing what we could have been? But she's my friend. I'm here for her and for Anna. But I can't deny that I still have feelings for you. It's been a struggle to keep them buried deep inside me."

Charles sighed, his expression a mix of sadness and guilt. "Rebecca, you know I care about you deeply. But we made a commitment to Charlotte, and I want to honor that."

Rebecca's voice quivered with emotion. "I never intended for this to happen, Charles. I never imagined that we would share such a deep connection. But since Anna's birth, I've grown even closer to you. It's hard seeing you with Anna, hard to hold her and not wonder what it would have been like if Anna was mine. It's tearing me apart."

Charles reached out, placing a comforting hand on Rebecca's arm. "I understand, Rebecca. We've been through so much together. But we must be strong and resist these feelings. Our loyalty lies with Charlotte and our commitment to my family and my marriage."

The words hung in the air, heavy with unspoken desire. Charlotte's heart skipped a beat as a sudden wave of disbelief and betrayal washed over her. She had trusted Charles implicitly, and Rebecca had become like family to them. Yet here they were, discussing their feelings for one another. Charles was her one and only love, but it made her chest tighten, thinking of Charles being with someone else. Worse, it was with her only friend. Charlotte's heart pounded in her chest, a mixture of anger, hurt, and confusion swirling inside her. How could they have let it come to this?

Taking a deep breath, Charlotte composed herself and silently retreated from her spying post. She needed time to process what she had overheard. Besides, listening in on such a private conversation felt intrusive, which was odd since it was her house and her husband, though at the moment, neither felt like hers.

Her feet took her downstairs and into the hallway on their own accord. She was so distracted she didn't notice the whispers growing from the shadows until something hissed her name. She stopped in midstride, her back foot resting on her toes. Charlotte's eyes darted around the spacious hall, looking for who – or what – called out to her.

The late afternoon sun cast long shadows across the walls, but there was no one she could see. She could hear them, though, like a hive of bees buzzing inside the walls. She rolled back on her rear foot, her body wanting to back away while her mind still tried to puzzle out what she was hearing.

One of the shadows moved, making her jump. She immediately tried to rationalize what she saw, straining to dream up some logical explanation for why the shadow did what it did. She wondered if it was caused by a tree swaying in the wind, but the shadow hadn't drifted, but had snapped out and back, like a cat pouncing on a bird. As her mind spun trying to explain it, the shadow moved again. This time, though, it didn't simply slide across the wall. It stepped out into the middle of the hall, somehow corporeal and not at the same time. Every muscle in Charlotte's body grew tight like a guitar string on the verge of snapping, ready to run at a moment's notice. She didn't blink, her eyelids locked open as wide as they could go. The shape before her was like a wax figure left out in the sun, vaguely human but melted and distorted, lacking any features or details. The thing took a tentative step forward as if it wasn't sure it wouldn't sink through the floor, but its second step was more confident, and its third more confident still.

Charlotte tried to turn and run while still keeping her eyes locked on the formless man, but her body could only twist so far. When her head snapped around to face the direction she was running, she jerked to a stop. Another shadow rose from the wall at the other end of the hall. She was pinned in. Could she just run through them?

They were incorporeal, like charcoal ghosts, but the thought of touching one, let alone being engulfed by one as she passed through it, filled her with dread. As the desperate idea of somehow running past one crossed her mind almost as fast as she could dismiss it as insane, the shadow-things reached out with their arms. They covered the width of the hall, casting like the long shadows they were made of, lacking any distinct features such as elbows or wrists. The forms were lopsided and wrong, one shoulder drooping like it was dislocated, one arm longer than the other. Charlotte felt a chill run down her spine, her bare arms breaking out in goosebumps. She thought it was just a sense of dread. It wasn't until she saw her breath in the air that she realized the temperature was dropping, as if the shadow-things were sucking in warmth as well as light.

Her only avenue of escape was a door to the side that led into the manor's library. As she darted for it, the creatures reached to the wall, their arms again becoming shadows as they slid along wood paneling toward her. She shoved open the door and bolted inside, throwing it closed behind her as one arm slid around the door frame. The arm dissipated like smoke where it was cut off by the door. Charlotte stepped back, her eyes locked on sunlight gleaming under the door. For a moment, nothing happened, and she dared to believe she had escaped. Then the shadow arms came sliding under the bottom of the closed door, slowly, like black water being spilled out in the hall. She turned, ready to bolt to the other end of the library, but froze. The other end of the library was made of gleaming panels of glass, letting in the orange light of dusk, and casting a grid of shadows from the window frames on the floor. It felt like staring out over a mind field, but on the other side of the room were the arced iron and glass French doors that led out to the courtyard.

Something tugged at the hem of her dress. Charlotte glanced down to see smoke-like fingers rising up from the two-dimensional arm painted on the floor. She reached down, grabbed her dress, and yanked it free. She didn't have a choice. Aiming for the squares of pale light, she sprinted for the door. Arms rose up from the grid of shadows, reaching for her. She felt them catch her dress, grasp her legs, and while she pulled free each time, it slowed her momentum. Then, one hand latched to her ankle, tripping her. She fell flat to the ground. The impact forced all the air out of her chest, but adrenaline fueled her. With the world spinning, she pushed herself up off the floor, but hands reached up from all around her and pulled her back down. She kicked and screamed, but for arms made of nothing, they were incredibly strong. Worse, they were cold, so cold they burned wherever they touched bare skin. Charlotte screamed in pain and panic. She was going to die. Worse, they would go after Anna next, and there was nothing she could do to stop it.

The French doors flew open. Charlotte looked up to see someone backlit by the dying light. Something round with dangling feathers hung from his outstretched hand, as a deep voice shouted, "*Mahsh!*"

A blinding light filled the room, bathing her in warmth reminiscent of that from a summer sun. The cold, dark shadows blew away like sand in the wind, the little bits popping and sparking into oblivion. Charlotte took in a breath as if she just surfaced from the bottom of the ocean. The skin where those things had touched her stung, the skin an angry red and threatening to blister, cycling from pain to shocked numbness back to pain.

The bright light faded with the shadows, leaving red and green spots dancing in her vision. As they faded away, she looked up to see her savior. He stepped into the library, the ambient light highlighting his reddish-brown skin. He had a prominent nose, but not in an unattractive way. His hair was a sleek black, combed back and styled in place. He looked young and fit, though he wore the clothes of a doddering old college professor, complete with leather patches on his tweed jacket. He knelt and offered her a hand. As she took it, she felt the calluses that didn't belong to a person who spent his life with books, but to a man who was no stranger to hard work. Something dangling from his neck gleamed in the setting sun like a spider web spun with silver thread and beads of bright blue turquoise.

"Hello," he said in a deep, monotone voice that seemed out of place for a man so young. "I've come to help. I'm Shayan Lightfoot, adjunct professor of anthropology at - "

"I'm sure your resume is impressive," Charlotte said, cutting him off, "but my daughter, my husband." After a breath's delay, she added, "My friend."

Rebecca didn't feel much like a friend at the moment. The conversation Charlotte eavesdropped on echoed in her thoughts, making her face flush with a mix of jealousy and anger. It wasn't even that Rebecca harbored feelings for her husband. That Charlotte could understand and forgive. She couldn't help but love Charles, so it wasn't hard to imagine someone else also loving him. What upset her was the secrecy. How could Rebecca have hidden this from her? Rebecca was supposed to be her friend. She told Rebecca her secrets and deepest feelings – well, except for anything regarding the old woman and her cryptic warnings. To think Rebecca didn't trust her in turn caused Charlotte's chest to tighten. The muscles in her hands started to ache from being clenched so long and so tightly. She relaxed her grip to see the impressions of her nails left in her hands.

"Mrs. Sloan?" Professor Lightfoot said, calling her out of her thoughts.

"Yes, sorry," Charlotte said. "We need to save them before those things, whatever they are, go after them. Go after Anna."

Lightfoot gave a curt nod. "Of course, though your daughter is perfectly safe, at least for now. They need her alive for the last rite."

"I don't understand," Charlotte said. "What is this last rite? What were those things?"

"We don't have time for me to tell you the full story now," Professor Lightfoot said. "What's important is that those shadow creatures are not from this world. According to legend, they view our world as an abomination. They want nothing more than to eliminate all of creation, and the last rite is the final piece that will allow them to enter our world to do just that."

"And my daughter?" Anna asked.

"I can't tell you why," the Professor said, "but your family line is the only one that can perform the last rite."

"Can't?" Charlotte asked. "Or won't?"

"I honestly do not know," the Professor said, though there was . . . what? A nearly imperceptible hesitation, a tightening of his lips, the pinching of his neck muscles . . . they all told Charlotte there was something he was keeping to himself. Was he lying? She didn't think so, but there was something. A suspicion, maybe?

He was right about one thing, however. They didn't have time to discuss it. Her husband and Rebecca were still in danger. "I left Rebecca and Charles in the nursery with the baby. This way."

She led Lightfoot into the hall, but he froze after a few steps. "What is it?"

He sniffed the air. "Was there a woman here earlier?"

Charlotte took a sniff herself. At first, she didn't notice anything, but then she picked up a faint hint of roses. "The photographer." When Lightfoot said nothing, Charlotte tugged on his sleeve. "What is it?"

Slowly, as if still forming the thought, he said, "I don't think she was a real photographer."

Before Charlotte could question him further, Professor Lightfoot held up his talisman and headed down the hall. The hall was in deeper relief now, more than could be explained by the setting sun. It was as if a giant hand reached up to grab the sun from the sky. Every long shadow was a potential hiding place for these new enemies, but she had no choice. She had to save her husband, her friend, and her daughter. She retraced her steps to the foyer and to the stairwell when she heard a scream, followed by Anna's cry. Throwing aside caution and Professor Lightfoot's attempts to stop her, she ran up the stairs with a determination only a desperate mother could have.

Charlotte burst through the door into the nursery. Rebecca curled her body over Anna, who cried in fear and confusion. Charles was trying to beat off more of those shadow creatures like he was putting out flames. After feeling those icy fingers on her own skin, Charlotte could relate, but she also knew how futile it was. She looked behind her to see Professor Lightfoot catching up to her. He held aloft his charm and said the same word as before. Again, the shadows dissipated like ash, but instead of the little particles popping into oblivion, they swirled and started to coalesce.

"We need to leave," Professor Lightfoot said. "They're growing stronger."

Charlotte stood frozen for a moment, her concern divided between her husband and her infant daughter. Rebecca showed no hesitation. With Anna in her arms, she went to Charles's side and knelt by him. She rested one hand on his shoulder. "Are you okay?"

He reached up and laid his hand on hers. A spike of jealousy stabbed Charlotte's heart as Charles locked eyes with Rebecca. It was only there and gone for a second, but in that brief moment, Charlotte could see it all – the love, guilt, desire, and shame. All of it. Then the moment passed, and they were on their feet.

"What's going on?" Charles asked, his eyes narrowed at the stranger, Professor Lightfoot. "Who is this?"

"We don't have time," Professor Lightfoot said, nodding to the shadow particles drifting in the air toward one another. "We need to leave."

Charles and Rebecca made their way to the hall, stepping around the reforming shadows like they were a nest of vipers. Hands reached out to them, but they didn't have the strength they had before . . . for now. Charlotte looked away from her husband and friend, very purposefully training her gaze on Professor Lightfoot. "What do we do? Where do we go?"

"I need to get you to the Order," Professor Lightfoot said. "We can make plans from there, but right now, we're in grave danger."

Charlotte looked at the shadows pulling themselves out of the darkness of the floor like creatures emerging from a bog. "How are they getting stronger?"

"Someone is feeding them," Professor Lightfoot said. "Come quickly, and stay close."

Professor Lightfoot held out his charm like a lantern as the others huddled behind him. The shadows swirled around them, trying to keep their form as Lightfoot's charm fought to dissipate them. Charlotte could hear the things hiss, though whether in anger or in pain, she couldn't tell.

"What do you mean someone is feeding them?" Charlotte asked.

"The rites open our world to them, each rite cracking it open a little more," Professor Lightfoot said. "Performing the rites funnels energy from our world to theirs. It's how they are able to take form, such as it is."

"Who would do this?" Charlotte asked. "Why?"

"As far as who, I can think of several people and organizations that could be culpable," Lightfoot said. "As to why, the forces in the other world can only come to this world if someone on our end lets them in, so the beings on the other side offer whatever they can to entice someone on our side to do so. Power, knowledge, whatever their short-sighted puppet on our side desires."

"Who in their right mind would be that short-sighted?" Charlotte asked.

Lightfoot averted his eyes. In a dark tone, he murmured, "You'd be surprised."

"I'm afraid to ask," Charlotte asked, "but what do they feed them?"

Lightfoot didn't reply, but the way the muscles clenched as he looked away made her grateful for not getting an answer.

Without warning, Professor Lightfoot froze. Charlotte looked over his shoulder, trying to figure out why, afraid of seeing some new horror coming their way. Instead, the hallway was clear. The shadows were retreating, melting away like snow on the first day of spring.

Or the way the ocean recedes before a coming tidal wave.

"Something bad is coming, isn't it?" Charlotte asked.

Professor Lightfoot didn't answer but sprinted down the hall. Charlotte raced after him, a reluctant Charles and Rebecca behind her. A weak and out-of-breath Charles gasped, "Where are we going? This is my home! I'm not running away!"

"That is currently not an option," Lightfoot called back over his shoulder. "We need to find the person performing the rite to seal the gate, or none of us will survive what comes next."

"What are we looking for?" Charlotte asked.

However, as they exited the house's front door, the answer was obvious. The large circular driveway was awash in a red and yellow glow from dozens of candles. Still, their light paled compared to the unnatural fountain of ethereal energy coming from the center of the driveway. The shadow things all stood in a circle like sentries, guarding a single woman kneeling on the ground. She had long jet-black hair and tanned skin not that different than Professor Lightfoot's complexion. Several of the candles held down rolls of parchment, with other cylindrical cases lying alongside her. Symbols and letters from an alphabet she couldn't recognize were scrawled along the smooth pavement in red. She wanted to tell herself it was paint, but the salty copper smell told her it couldn't be anything but blood. Her sleeves were rolled up, exposing her bare arms and the many cuts that explained where the woman got the ink for her ritualistic markings. Blood dripped down the woman's arms. Laying in front of her, as if at a place of honor, was a long knife with an ornate handle, the blade edge glistening with fresh blood. The woman in the circle chanted something in a language Charlotte didn't recognize, but with the vigor of a person possessed, her eyes clamped shut in concentration.

An icy chill ran down Charlotte's spine. It took her a moment to recognize the woman as the photographer. Her equipment bag sat open outside the circle. She had brought the candles and that knife with her. Brought it into Charlotte's house. Brought it near her baby. The chanting woman had planned this from the beginning.

From behind her, still in Rebecca's arms, Anna started to cry. A mother could always tell what her baby's cry meant, could tell the difference between crying out of hunger or from fear or pain, but this was a new cry. Still, Charlotte knew what it meant because she felt it too. Whatever came from that geyser of energy, spewing from a hole in reality, was wrong.

"You feel it, don't you?" Professor Lightfoot said. "Your daughter as well."

The woman in the center of the markings stopped her chanting, opened her eyes, and looked up at them. "Shayan. Have you missed me?"

Charlotte looked from the kneeling woman to Professor Lightfoot. "You know her?"

"Once," Lightfoot said, "but no longer."

"I see you found both the key and the forge," the bleeding woman said.

"And you will have neither of them," Lightfoot said.

A humorless grin spread across the woman's face. She reached over, grabbed one of the cylindrical cases, popped off the top, and pulled out another rolled-up parchment stained yellow with age. The color drained from Professor Lightfoot's face as she rolled it out in front of her.

"Keme, no!" he gasped.

The woman – Keme, Charlotte presumed – ignored Lightfoot and began reading the scroll. Charlotte looked from Keme to Lightfoot, not understanding what was happening. She asked

Lightfoot, "What is she doing?"

"The third rite," Professor Lightfoot said to her. Then, to Keme, he shouted, "Keme! Stop! You don't know what you're doing!"

"Oh, for God's sake," Charles spat. He stomped past Lightfoot and marched towards the woman. Lightfoot reached out to grab him, trying to stop him, but Charles pushed him aside and stormed toward Keme. Before he could reach her, however, the shadows swarmed on him. Charlotte and Rebecca stood frozen in place, unable to do anything but stand in horror and watch Charles try in vain to swat away the incorporeal threats. Lightfoot held out his talisman and chanted the same word repeatedly, but the shadows were so much stronger now, drawing power through the opening to their world. Every repeat of the phrase from Lightfoot hit the shadow things like a strong ocean wave. Despite being pushed back they kept their form and held on to a screaming Charles. Charlotte could see his skin blistering from their ice-cold touch.

Then, in a moment of blind desperation, Rebecca ran to Charles, the man she loved, with Anna still in her arms! Charlotte yelled out to Rebecca to stop, but before she could rip Anna out of Rebecca's arms, she realized the shadow things floated back from Rebecca as if they found her repulsive.

No, not Rebecca. They were repelled by Anna. Because they needed her, Charlotte realized. She was the key to the last rite. The shadow things weren't afraid of Anna. They were afraid of hurting Anna, of damaging their key.

With Anna nestled in one arm, Rebecca hooked another under

Charles's arm and pulled him away from the shadow things. With Anna as her inadvertent talisman, the shadow creatures could do nothing but pull back and let them go. All the while, Keme maintained her chant.

The fire exploded into a gusher of flame as they wrapped around Keme. She leaned back, letting the flame coil around her, a look of rapture on her face. Lightfoot cried, "Keme! No!"

"What's happening?" Charlotte asked.

"The beings from the other side, they're coming over," Lightfoot said, "but they are without physical form as we know it." Then all color drained from his face as he said grimly, "So they need to create one out of what they find here."

As he said it, Keme's euphoria morphed into concern, then stark terror as the tendrils of green flame started to pinch - then tear – at her flesh. Charlotte looked away, not wanting to see, but the sounds of bones snapping and skin ripping painted a picture in her mind, more clear than her eyes ever could.

"We have to close the portal before it comes through," Professor Lightfoot shouted over the screams of the thing that used to be Keme. "Before it can complete creating a physical form to inhabit."

"How?" Charlotte asked.

"I . . . I'm not sure," Professor Lightfoot said. "I've only read about this."

Charlotte looked about for something to use, trying very hard not to look at the creature being pieced haphazardly together from the remnants of what used to be a person. A yard tool left out or a fallen tree branch, anything that could be used as a weapon or to close the portal. Then she spotted the heavy bird bath. She had no idea if it would work, but she couldn't think of anything else. She raced to the other side of the birdbath and pushed, but it was so heavy! It wouldn't budge.

"Help me!"

Charles, Rebecca, and Professor Lightfoot all ran to join her. All four of them shoved at the lip of the bird batch, Rebecca one-handed as she held Anna close to her. The top of the birdbath slipped off the plinth, tipping over and crashing to the ground. The marble shattered, and the water splashed out across the driveway. The cold and dirty water ran through the shadow creatures like they weren't there. The symbols of blood hissed as the water hit them, not entirely washing them away but smearing and distorting them. It was enough. The flames sputtered. The creature that was forming out of the parts torn from Keme cried out, but it was a very different scream than Keme's. It was more guttural, full of snarls and growls, more anger than pain. Charlotte braved a look at the partially formed creature in the damaged circle. As the green flames retreated, the mismatched chunks of meat collapsed to the ground in a wet splat, like a water-drenched marionette whose strings had been cut. The shadow creatures were sucked back into the opening. They clawed at the ground in vain but were all dragged back to wherever they came from.

And like that, it was over. The shadow creatures, the unearthly green flames, all of it. It was done. Lightfoot walked over to the remains of Keme and knelt. He stayed there with his head bowed as if in prayer. Charlotte walked over to him and laid a hand on his shoulder.

"She lost her way," Lightfoot said. "A long time ago. I hoped she would someday find her way back to me. I guess she never will now."

"I'm sorry," Charlotte said.

Lightfoot nodded, more to himself than to Charlotte. "I'm just not sure how to tell our children."

Charlotte pulled her hand back like he was on fire. "You and her? You were . . ."

After a very pregnant pause, Lightfoot answered, "Like I said, it was a long time ago. She was a different person then, but she was seduced by the promises of those from the other side."

"What?" Charlotte asked. "What could she possibly want that would be worth the end of the world?"

Lightfoot took a deep breath, then looked deep into Charlotte's eyes. "Our daughter. She wanted our daughter back. I tried to tell her, we needed to live for our two sons, but she couldn't get past the loss of our daughter."

Charlotte forced herself to look at the thing that used to be a person. The body was twisted and distorted out of shape, the skin – where there was still skin – blistered or burned to a charred black. Her face was melted, but her one remaining human eye stared out, frozen in terror.

"What happened?" she asked.

Lightfoot got to his feet. "A story for another time, perhaps. Right now, we have to plan our next move."

"Our next . . . but, it's over. The creatures are gone."

"Those who summoned them will try again," Lightfoot said. "We won this battle, but the war, as they say, is far from over. We need to hide you from them before they can try again."

"Where are we going to hide?" Charlotte asked. "How?"

"I don't know," Lightfoot said. "There are others I work with, a group dedicated to preventing the last rite from being performed. Together, maybe we can come up with a plan."

Charlotte looked over to where Rebecca knelt next to Charles. Anna was nuzzled in Rebecca's arms as if she belonged there. Without shifting her gaze, she said to Lightfoot, "The old woman. She said Charles and I could not have any more children. That I couldn't have any more children. It's like a curse, right?"

"Something like that, yes," Lightfoot said.

Charlotte walked over to Rebecca and Charles. They got to their feet, looking ashamed as if caught having an affair, which Charlotte supposed that, in a way, they had. Charlotte swallowed hard, stealing herself for what she had to do. "You need to take Anna and go."

"What are you talking about," Charles said. "I'm not leaving you. You're my wife."

"No," Charlotte said, looking at Rebecca and hoping the raging jealousy she felt didn't show. "Rebecca is your wife now."

The two of them looked at each other, then turned their puzzled looks back to Charlotte. "You want a divorce?" Charles asked. "Honey, whatever it is, we can talk . . ."

Charlotte held up a hand to stop him. "You need to take Anna and hide. She's not safe with me."

"That's ridiculous," Rebecca said. "You're her mother . . ."

"Not anymore," Charlotte said, rushing the words out before she lost her nerve. "They know I can't have any more children, but you can. You two can have as many children as you want. If Anna has a brother or a sister, they won't think she's the one they are looking for." She locked eyes with Rebecca. "As far as the rest of the world is concerned, you are Anna's mother. You and Charles can have another child, *must* have another child."

Rebecca was a storm of conflicting emotions. Dread, hope, and puzzlement all blurred together. Charles, however, was just confused. "Why?"

"Camouflage," Charlotte said. "You'll hide Anna in plain sight."

"Charlotte, I . . ." Charles began, but she touched his lips and shushed him.

"It's not that bad. I know you two have feelings for each other." It was getting harder for her to talk, her throat pinching as her eyes filled with tears. "You'll be happy together. And more importantly, you'll be safe."

Charles opened his mouth, but he couldn't form any words. Rebecca walked up and took Charlotte's hand. She nodded toward Professor Lightfoot. "Are you sure about this? Do you trust him?"

She looked at Lightfoot over her shoulder as if seeing him for the first time. She thought about this stranger who came from nowhere to save her daughter, sent to her by a mysterious old woman who shadowed her all her life. "Yes, I think I so."

Rebecca looked down at Anna and caressed her head. "I'll care for her as if she were my own. I promise."

"I know you will," Charlotte said.

"Do you want to hold her?" Rebecca asked. "One last time?"

Charlotte knew Rebecca meant it as a kindness, but it broke Charlotte's heart. She resisted the urge to take Anna in her arms, afraid that if she did, she wouldn't be able to let her go. And she had to let her go. For her daughter's safety, she had to leave her. With tears in her eyes, she turned and walked to Professor Lightfoot. He looked to her as if to ask if she were sure, but as Charlotte walked past without breaking stride, Lightfoot fell in behind her. The two left Charles, Rebecca, and Anna behind, never to see them again.

Anna closed the diary. There might be more to Charlotte's story, but it wouldn't be here. Rebecca had written everything down for Anna, recording the events so she could know the truth, but Rebecca never had the chance to share it with her. Anna caressed the book. It wasn't clear from the story's context how Rebecca knew parts of the story, parts where Charlotte was alone while Rebecca and her father were in the other room. Had Charlotte come to see Anna or checked up on her, giving Charlotte opportunity to fill Rebecca in on her part of the story? Was Charlotte still alive?

Anna sat down on the attic floor. So many questions were answered, but they only led to more questions. Who were the people after her mother – her *real* mother – and what was this last rite they talked about? How old was the old woman to have visited her mother all her life? The way Rebecca described the old woman, she was just the same as she was now. How was that possible?

It was weird thinking of her mother as *Rebecca*, but now in her mind, she had to distinguish the woman who raised her from the woman who gave birth to her. There was a strange dichotomy now, Rebecca being both her mother and an imposter, simultaneously. She caressed the book again, wondering if Rebecca meant this as a confession, if she felt guilty for taking her friend's child as her own. Maybe she felt angry, as if Charlotte was a cuckoo bird that hid her egg in another's nest. No, neither felt right, knowing what she knew of her mother and reading the diary she left behind. It wasn't written out of guilt or anger but out of love.

It was the act of a mother.

Anna tucked the book under the waistband of her pants. She stayed there in the attic for a while longer, rummaging through the trunk for anything she might have missed. There was a photo in an ornate white frame of her mother – her *biological* mother – standing by her father. It was their wedding photo. Her father looked dapper in his tuxedo, but Anna's eyes focused on the dress Charlette wore. It was the same one hanging in her father's closet. Putting the photo aside, Anna dove back into the chest. She found a newspaper clipping dated over twenty years ago about a photographer found dead and his camera equipment stolen in an apparent robbery-gone-bad, but Anna could connect the dots. Keme had killed the photographer and impersonated him to. . . what, exactly? Kill her mother? Sacrifice Anna for this last rite thing?

Anna closed the trunk. She wanted to take it with her, but it was too heavy to drag it through the woods back to her car. She debated taking some of the photos, but she decided it was best to have Mark get it for her when he delt with the rest of the assets in the house – their father's "estate". She also wondered if she should take Charlotte's wedding dress. Her father must have saved it for her. She could imagine an alternate universe where she planned to marry Daniel, and her father presented her with not only the dress but the truth about her mother. As much as she wanted it, she decided to leave it behind. Being weighted down as she hiked back through the woods to the car would leave her vulnerable. She'd add it to the list of things she'd ask Mark to get for her. The diary would have to do. For now.

Anna climbed down the ladder out of the attic. However, as she made her way down the main stairs, she got a clear view through the front windows and across the driveway. At the far end of the driveway, Anna caught sight of someone in a dark business suit. He stood where the driveway connected to the main road as if waiting for someone.

As if waiting for her.

Anna descended the stairs quietly, even though there was no way the man could hear her from outside and so far away. Without turning around, she crept her way to the back door. She edged her way to the window and peeked out, but no one was there. As she returned to the forest path, each painful red mark on her arm reminded her of the long and arduous hike to the house. At the time, every scratch made her wonder if she had been paranoid. Now, she realized she was right to be cautious. She didn't know who the man in the suit was, but it was clear the old woman was right. Someone was looking for her and Bethany, and they needed to stay hidden.

By the time she reached the car, the sun had set. Miles away from city streets and buildings, she only had the moonlight to see by. She crouched while sneaking her way up to the tree line, but there was no sign of anyone watching for her. At least, none she could see in the dark. She supposed if anyone was hiding in the trees or even in a car parked down the road with night-vision goggles, she'd never see them. Just in case, she stayed low as she crept to the driver's side door, ducked down as she opened it and kept the headlights off as she started it up. Keeping the lights off, she released the brake and let the car coast down the road. She strained to see in the near-pitch blackness of night without the car's lights. She went nearly a mile before the fear of getting hit by an oncoming car outweighed her fear of being seen by someone who may or may not be out there looking for her.

She looped around her brother's place several times, looking for any signs of people staked out looking for her. On her third loop around the block, she was confident no one was there. She parked the car some distance away and walked back. Between hiking through the woods, all the searching in the attic, and now the march up to her brother's place, she was exhausted. Her feet ached, and her calves were tight. She wanted nothing more than to sit down and rest. Instead, she knocked on her brother's door, and Mark opened it.

"Mommy!" Bethany shouted with glee. Anna knelt as Bethany

ran to her and jumped into her waiting arms, almost knocking Anna over. It was as if Bethany was one of those wireless battery chargers for her cell phone, giving Anna a boost of energy. After squeezing Anna as hard as her little arms could, she danced in place like water on a hot skillet, too excited to hold still. "Uncle Mark and I had so much fun! He has video games! And we colored! And he let me have beer!"

Anna's eyes popped open at that last one, and she shot Mark a look. He let out a sly grin. "Root beer. Don't worry, I'm not that bad an uncle."

Anna let Bethany lead her into the house, talking a mile a minute about her day. Mark beamed with pride at being such a fun uncle as Bethany showed Anna every video game they played, some of which earned Mark a scornful glare when Anna noticed the title or rating on the cover. Then she showed Anna the coloring she had done, and the warmth Anna had been enjoying evaporated.

Printed on the first page of a dime-store coloring book was a thick-lined drawing of a cartoon character. Bethany's crayon marks scrawled across the lines, but they did a fair job filling in the shapes with color. Drawn all around the white space of the picture, however, Bethany had scribbled in black shapes, each with the vague form of a head and two arms coming out of elongated torsos. As Bethany flipped the pages of the coloring book, showing her mother every page she had colored with the kind of pride only a young child could have, Anna's dread deepened. Her fingertips turned cold, as if the pages were carved from ice. On every page, Bethany had used a black crayon to draw dark shadows around the cartoon characters.

"Baby?" It was hard for Anna to get the words out, her chest feeling tight and making it hard to breathe. "Why did you draw these?"

Bethany shrugged. "Everyone has shadows."

Anna swallowed her fear. Bethany was too engrossed in showing off her artwork to notice, but Anna was trying to keep from crying at every turn of the page. She was grateful when Bethany reached the end of the book with a cheerful, "And that's all!"

"Very good, baby," Anna said.

Some of her dread must have seeped into her words because Bethany's expression darkened. "What's wrong, Mommy?"

Anna ran her fingers through Bethany's light brown hair and forced a smile. "Nothing, baby, just had a long day. I'm tired."

Bethany thought about it for a moment, then wrapped her arms around Anna and squeezed her as hard as she could. Then she leaned back. "Did that make it all better?"

Anna smiled. It did make her feel better, though it couldn't completely chase away the idea that those dark creatures which had hunted Charlotte weren't hiding in every shadow. Had Bethany seen the same shadow creatures? Had she somehow picked it up from Anna while she read her mother's – plural, she guessed – diary like some kind of psychic radio? Anna wasn't sure which answer made her more uneasy.

A knock came at the door, and Anna jumped. Mark held up his hands. "Whoa! Jumpy, much? It's okay. I ordered a pizza."

"Pizza!" Bethany cried out, jumping up and down.

Despite Mark's reassurances, Anna's muscles tightened, and

her pulse quickened, expecting some unknown assailant, or worse, one of those shadow creatures waiting on the other side of the door. As Mark swung the door open with no concern, she saw a pimply-faced boy wearing a T-shirt and ball cap, each sporting the same pizza-themed logo and holding the flat cardboard box of a pizza.

After an exciting day meeting her uncle and with a belly full of pizza, Bethany lay fast asleep on the couch. Anna sat next to her, caressing her hair. Mark had pulled up one of the dining room chairs and sat opposite them. "She's a good kid. You did good there, sis."

Anna smiled. "Thanks."

Mark leaned forward. "So, you find out anything about . . . whatever it is you're trying to figure out?"

Anna looked up at her brother. How much should she share with him? Should he know that they're not really brother and sister, that they had the same father but came from different mothers? She recalled what Charlotte called her brother before he was even conceived.

Camouflage.

Mark must have read something in her hesitation. "What, am I adopted or something?"

Anna cracked a smile. "Who would choose to have you on purpose?"

Mark chuckled, but then his face grew stern. "Seriously, though? What's going on? C'mon, I want to help, but I can't protect you if I don't know what I'm protecting you from?"

Anna thought back to what Mark had told her at the diner,

about what their father had told him. *Always look out for your sister.* At the time, she thought it the words of a father who thought of his daughter as the fairer sex, of someone who needed to be saved, of someone who couldn't possibly take care of herself. After what she had learned today, maybe it wasn't her that her father was concerned about, but the world.

Anna reached behind her and pulled out Rebecca's diary. She handed it to Mark. "Here, read this."

Mark took the book from her. "What's this about?"

"Our family," Anna said, "and the burden we have to carry."

Mark gave her an odd look, but Anna wasn't worried. Mark would read the book, then he'd understand. Anna felt hope for the first time since the old woman had intercepted her in the parking lot, before she could tell Daniel she was pregnant with Bethany. For the first time in a long time, she wasn't alone.

She had her family again.

EPILOGUE

Nick peered out the window from the small apartment he shared with the local agent. When given the assignment, he was concerned that a Caucasian in Angeles City would stand out. Considering his job was to go unnoticed, being an American in the Philippines wasn't what he considered low profile. Then they paired him with a local, a young Pinay woman who could have been his youngest sister – if Ashley had lived. He felt like a pervert hanging around with a woman almost half his age, but apparently, that was how he went unseen in Angeles City, a city filled with middle-aged Western men hanging around with young Filipino women who were barely adults.

"She seems happy," his partner said.

Nick glanced over at Isa, who peeked out from behind the drapes. She stared down at the street below, watching their target walk by. Said target went by the name May, but according to the file given to him by Professor Lightfoot, that was an alias. Her aunt had even more aliases, a list almost as long as her unnaturally long lifespan. Nick walked over to the window and peered down at the street below.

"She seems to like that fishball she's eating," Nick said.

"What?"

Isa bolted from the window to the nightstand of their one-room apartment, pulled out a pair of binoculars, ran to his window, and shoved him aside. Ignoring any pretense of subtlety, she aimed the binoculars toward May.

"What? Those fishball things are good," Nick said. "I just never saw her eat one before."

"You never saw her eat anything before," Isa said. "*Manananggals* can't eat human food."

"What? That can't . . . let me see." Nick took the binoculars from Isa and stared down at their target, the supposed *manananggal*. All he saw was an ordinary Filipino woman eating as she walked toward her home.

No, he was looking, but he wasn't seeing. He had to remember his training from the Order. He had to look past the surface. She wasn't a normal Filipino woman. She was an exquisitely beautiful woman. In fact, it was safe to say she was the most beautiful woman in sight, possibly the most beautiful woman he had ever seen. That kind of beauty wasn't proof of the supernatural, but it did suggest it. She wasn't just eating the local street food. She savored every bite like she hadn't tasted anything so decadent in her life.

"Have we been watching the wrong target this whole time?" Nick asked, running his hand through his short-cropped silver hair. "These baby-eating things, what happens if they eat normal food?"

"From the stories I've been told," Isa said, "they get violently ill."

Nick lowered the binoculars and shot a glance at his partner. "Stories? We don't know? You've never seen one of these many-gal things?"

"No, I've never seen a *manananggal*," Isa said, pronouncing the name slowly and distinctly. "You know how you know I haven't seen a *manananggal*? I'm still alive."

He glanced back out the window. May looked to be many things, but dangerous wasn't one of them. Still, this was a change in her behavior. He stepped away from the window and went to the nightstand on his side. Isa and Nick shared the bed, but only to keep up appearances. They hot-racked it – one person sleeping while the other took a shift watching out for any signs of this baby-eater thing in the night. They may share the bed, but they each took a nightstand for themselves to store some personal gear. Nick pulled open the drawer and fished out his laptop. The laptop was bulkier than one bought at a consumer electronics store. The Order got him a rugged piece designed to survive out in the field, including a satellite modem. He sat the laptop on the edge of the bed, opened it up, and hit the power button. No sooner did the boot screen light up did Isa reach over and slam the laptop shut.

"What are you doing?" Isa hissed.

His face went slack. "Filing a report. Standard Order protocol — "

"No," she said. "Lightfoot said no records."

"What?" Nick was shocked mute for a moment. That didn't sound like the Professor Lightfoot he knew. "The Order has procedures, and I've followed them since you were in diapers . . ."

Nick trailed off, his own words haunting him. He hadn't thought about those days in years. Those were dark days, going through the motions of living and wondering why he should bother. The last happy day of his life was when his family dropped him off at college. His parents were so proud of him. Rachel was being a moody teenager, and Ashley . . . just thinking about poor Ashley made his eyes well up.

Since you were in diapers.

Ashley was still in diapers. He would never know for sure why his father drove off the road into that utility pole, but the police theorized his father had nodded off while driving. He kind of hoped it was true. If they were all asleep, then their deaths might have been painless.

Pulling Nick back into the moment, Isa leaned in closer and spoke in a stiff staccato. "Lightfoot said no."

"Professor Lightfoot has been in the order longer than almost anyone alive. He recruited me while I was in college shortly after - "

Nick cut himself off, losing himself in the memory. Though it happened over two decades ago, it hit him as if the tragedy of his family's death was yesterday. He almost didn't make it that first year of college, his studies suffering due to grief and the never-ending problems in dealing with the family's estate. As a nineteen-year-old college freshman, he was unprepared for the hassles of liquidating assets and managing funerals. The biggest impact on his studies, however, was the loss of direction. He was left asking himself, *Why am I doing this? What's the point?*

Then one day, while sitting in the cafeteria picking at his food, he heard the chair next to him drag across the tile floor. Nick looked up to see a professor he didn't recognize take a seat at Nick's table as if the spot was reserved for him. He sat stiff-backed, but despite his rigid posture he gave Nick a warm smile. His hair was still black in those days, not yet turned grey, and his face lacked the deep wrinkles and creases the professor had today.

"I'm Professor Lightfoot," the man said. Before Nick could bring himself to reply, Lightfoot nodded and added, "And you're Nick. I understand you've had a personal tragedy. I'm sorry for your loss."

Nick remembered looking back at his plate and saying nothing, but was that right? He was young, he was hurt, and he was angry. If he had said anything under his breath, Lightfoot was kind enough to ignore it, and Nick was too embarrassed by it to record it in his memories.

"I've been where you are, son," Professor Lightfoot said. "I've come to offer you help."

Nick dropped his fork to his plate. "You can help? You can bring my parents back? My sisters?"

As an adult recalling this conversation, Nick would have been way less patient with his younger self than Lightfoot was. Nick wanted to reach back through time and slap his younger self, but Professor Lightfoot showed only patience. "I would if I could, son. I really would. I can, however, offer you something else you're lacking."

"Like what?" Nick spat.

"Like help with your legal and financial issues," Professor Lightfoot said. "I work with an organization that can help you settle your family's affairs, restructure your debts to pay for their funeral costs and keep you in school." Then Professor Lightfoot leaned forward. "More importantly, I can give you purpose. This organization I work for, we work to protect people."

"What, like Greenpeace or something?" Nick asked skeptically.

"Something like that. We're trying to save more than whales, however." Professor Lightfoot pulled out a business card and slid it across the table to Nick. "Right now, you're rudderless. It's hard to move forward with your life when you have no direction. We can give you that."

Professor Lightfoot didn't wait for Nick to reply. He stood up and turned to leave, but Nick called out, "Why? What is it to you? Why do you care?"

When Professor Lightfoot turned back, his smile wasn't as

bright anymore. It was a mask hiding his own tragedy. Nick recognized it from having to wear his own fake smile for so many months. Professor Lightfoot and Nick had an understanding at that moment, both knowing the other's pain, even if Nick didn't know the details of the Professor's.

Nick took a long, calming breath, bringing him back to the moment. He looked to Isa and said, "Back when I was initiated, we used to joke that Lightfoot had been in the Order so long he knew the Mad Arab himself. Lightfoot wouldn't break protocol. He wrote the protocols for crying out loud! Why would he want to keep this off the books?"

Isa shrugged. "Only one reason I can think of. He doesn't want someone to know about our *manananggal*."

"That's crazy," Nick said. "We're a secret organization. Who would we tell?"

"Someone within the Order," Isa said.

On the small table where they ate their meals, a cell phone rang. Isa and Nick looked at each other, each waiting for the other to get the phone. Isa gritted her teeth, walked to the table, and picked up the phone. "Hello?" After a pause, she added, "I recommend the tilapia. It's fresh."

Nick tensed. That was the countersign, confirming their identity to the caller. Nick didn't know who Isa was talking to, but he knew whoever was on the other end of the line was a member of the Order.

"I'm sorry. Can you repeat that?" Isa asked into the phone,

though her eyes were locked on Nick. Nick mouthed a silent "What?" but Isa held up a finger. "You can't be serious . . . yes. Yes, sir, I understand. It will be done."

Isa put down the phone. Nick asked, "What is it? Do they want us to move on the monster? The *manna-gal* thing?"

For a moment, Isa just stood there, her facial muscles twitching as she tried to organize her thoughts. Then she said, "You're not going to believe this."

Nick and Isa walked together across the street to where the monster lived. Isa was skittish, torn between not wanting to go anywhere near the baby-eating monster but also not wanting to wait. It was midday, and it was as safe as it was going to be. According to Isa, the monster, this *manananggal*, was, like most monsters, more deadly at night.

"How should we approach this?" Isa asked.

"You're asking me?" Nick said. "You're the local expert."

"If it was up to me, we wouldn't be doing this at all," Isa growled. She kept her voice low so not to be heard by the crowd, but it forced Nick to lean over to hear her. "You don't talk to a *manananggal*, you run from it."

"You said yourself, you've never seen one," Nick said. "Maybe the stories are . . . embellished?"

Isa stopped and dragged Nick to the entrance of an alley. With her back to the crowd, she pulled her shirt collar to the side, exposing the round scars of ancient puncture wounds. "When I was a girl, an *aswang* jumped me as I was carrying water from the stream. I barely escaped with my life. My father heard me screaming and came to save me. Three days later, my father died from his wounds."

Nick swallowed hard. "I'm sorry."

Isa let go of her shirt, letting it drape back over her scars as she stepped into Nick's face. "I don't want your sympathy. I want you to hear me. That was a small *aswang*. That was nothing compared to a *manananggal*."

The way Nick had come to understand it, the *aswang* were a class of monsters here in the Philippines, to which the *manananggal* belong to. According to the stories, however, the *manananggal* was one of the most dangerous. If *aswang* were sharks, the *manananggal* would be a Great White.

"She's a killer," Isa said.

"We've been watching her for weeks," Nick said. "She seems friendly enough. The people like her."

"They don't know what she is," Isa growled.

"Then we use that," Nick said. "We stay in public view. That way, she can't act without blowing her cover."

"Then what?"

Nick shrugged. "Then we talk."

Isa's neck tightened as the thought of having a casual chat with such a vile monster caused her physical discomfort. Nick wasn't thrilled with the plan either, but their job had been to keep an eye on this creature, so Nick felt he knew her quite well. He'd seen her be kind, seen her rush off to help save a missing boy, and seen that boy home safe and sound with a grateful family. It was hard to imagine the kind, beautiful woman ripping herself in half at night as she devoured unborn children.

They approached her door, knocked, then took several steps back. They both wanted to ensure they could be seen by those passing by. Being in public was their only protection. The door opened, and Nick was taken aback by her stunning beauty.

"May I help you?" she asked.

Nick stood frozen, mesmerized by her beauty, until Isa nudged him with an elbow. "Uh, yes, sorry. We've come to talk."

The woman, May, cocked an eyebrow. "About what?"

The two humans exchanged looks, steeling their nerves, before facing the monster posing as a gorgeous woman. "We're part of a secret order tasked with defending humanity from supernatural threats."

May's eyes hardened. "Supernatural threats? Like me, I suppose?"

"And worse," Isa said, "if you can imagine that."

May didn't move. Her expression didn't change. Yet somehow, she looked like a tiger ready to pounce. Without so much as twitching an eyebrow, she went from the most attractive woman Nick had ever met to the most terrifying thing in existence. "So, you are here to kill me?"

"No," Nick said. Again, he and Isa exchanged looks as if one of them would tell the other this was all a big mistake. Then Nick turned back to May. "We're here to ask for your help."

Again, May didn't move a finger, but all of the tension melted away. Nick felt like a gun was just pulled away from his head. "Help with what?"

"Saving the world," Nick said.

178

ABOUT THE AUTHOR

Chad Robert Morgan was born and raised in California. He served in the Navy as a Hospital Corpsman and worked his way through college as a vocational nurse. As well as writing, Chad works in the video game industry. He currently lives in southern California with his wife Carol and his youngest son Alexander.

www.ingramcontent.com/pod-product-compliance
Lightning Source LLC
LaVergne TN
LVHW041705060526
838201LV00043B/583